Publisher's note. Taking a train full of currency or capturing a Spanish treasure ship is nothing compared to the greatest theft in history—when the captain of a company of English archers and his men stole the entire treasury and religious relics of the world's greatest and richest empire and escaped to Cornwall with chests and chests of gold coins and priceless relics. This is part of the exciting and action-packed story of how it happened and, in particular, what happened afterward to affect the people involved.

More specifically, this is another of the "good reads" in an exciting and action-packed saga about an Englishman who rose to become the battle-scarred captain of a company of English archers and fought his way to wealth and recognition, and forever changed England, by showing how men who had not been born into the nobility, or as the by-blows of churchmen and rich merchants, could rise through trade and the military, and then buy themselves into the nobility or the upper reaches of the church if they fancied a title or needed one for their dealings with foreigners.

The other books in this exciting medieval saga are also available on Kindle. They can all be found as eBooks on Amazon and some of them are in print. Search for *Martin Archer saga.*

The parchments on which this novel is based were found some years ago in a trunk buried under a pile of rubble in the Bodelian Library basement. What follows in this exciting story was mostly taken from the parchments written by and about William Courtenay, born in a farming village in Kent, describing his experiences and battles as he rose in the years after King Richard's crusade to become the captain of a company of English archers based in Cornwall. Other sources were parchments describing the activities and thoughts of his priestly brother Thomas, his son George, and several of his key lieutenants and sergeants.

All in all, this is an exciting story about the early beginnings of Europe's first standing army since the Romans, and how the first of the great merchant companies of Britain was formed—the archers of Cornwall.

Only one thing is clear, men haven't changed very much since those early days, if at all.

The Magna Carta Decision

A novel of medieval England

The Background.

Things were tense in England in the spring of 1215, and particularly in London and at Windsor Castle. A civil war was coming and both King John and his rebellious barons were gathering their forces and trying to hire mercenaries to supplement them. The rebel barons had taken London and their troops had been reinforced by French knights sent by

Prince Louis of France, heir to the French throne and a possible replacement for John. The rebel barons had also taken Lincoln and one of their leaders, the Earl of Devon, had a firm hold on Exeter.

King John wanted peace, at least he wanted it until he could strengthen his remaining forces enough to destroy the rebel barons and seize their castles and lands. Accordingly, a few months earlier, the king had concentrated his forces at Windsor and begun playing for time by inviting a council of nobles and clergymen to assemble in Oxford, including some of the rebels, and advise him on how to restore peace to England.

Forming the council was an idle gesture and almost everyone knew it. Even so, Thomas, the priestly older brother of the captain of a company of archers based in Cornwall, and an archer himself as well as the bishop of church's poor, and thus priest-free, Cornwall diocese, had hurried to Oxford to make sure that the archers and Cornwall were protected from any decision that might embroil them in the conflict and, of course, to see if he could extract anything of benefit for his family and the archers.

Also on the council was Stephen Langton, the priest the king now accepted as the Archbishop of Canterbury after getting excommunicated by the Pope for initially not accepting him in order to sell the post to someone else. Langton had joined the council because he thought he could negotiate a permanent agreement between the king and the barons.

On the other hand, because they knew it was a meaningless exercise and didn't want to appear to be siding with either side, many of the men the king invited to join the council found one excuse or another not to show up. The council itself was presided over by the famed tournament jouster, and widely respected soldier, Sir William Marshal, the commander of the king's army, or else there would have been even fewer men in attendance.

It wasn't that the king wanted the council's advice. He didn't. The king was playing for time because he expected support to arrive from the Pope—which he reasonably expected because several years earlier he had pledged himself to be a tithe-paying vassal of the Pope and accepted Stephen Langton as the Archbishop of Canterbury. As a result of pledging his liege and tithes to the Pope, and accepting Langton, John's excommunication had been lifted and the barons lost some of their supporters.

But then, last summer, many of King John's supporters fell, or were captured, at the Battle of Bouvines in France. It had been fought, and lost, in an effort to regain the lands of King John's family in Normandy which had been lost years earlier as a result of a previous war with the French. The loss of so many of his supporters greatly reduced the number of men John could put into the field against his rebellious barons. It also effectively ended both the king's efforts to regain his family's ancestral estates in France and his ability to reward his supporters with some of those lands and the revenues they would produce.

The decisive and humiliating defeat of King John and his supporters in France increased the anger of England's barons and emboldened them. This occurred because King John had been forced to sue for peace, and, to get it, had agreed to pay compensation to both his allies and the French for their losses—and then couldn't pay any of them even though he had levied new taxes and scutages on his barons in an effort to raise the necessary coins.

Unfortunately for the king, instead of paying the new taxes to help the king pay for his latest defeat, the irate barons organized themselves into a military force under the king's sworn enemies, Robert FitzWalter and the Earl of Devon, and took control of London and Lincoln with the help of a large force of French knights. Devon and his men already hold Exeter. They were determined to replace John with someone, anyone, even the heir to the French throne if that's what it would take to gather a large enough army to defeat King John and put someone else on the throne.

Stephen Langton, the Archbishop of Canterbury, wanted peace and was attempting to mediate a solution to the tense dispute between the barons and the king even though he was a leading supporter of the rebels. Langton knew King John was playing for time, but thought that with enough prayers, threats of burning in purgatory, and craftiness, he might be able to cajole the barons and the king into a permanent agreement as to their respective rights and powers, a charter as they were called in those days. Accordingly, Langton volunteered to accompany the king when he went out of Windsor to meet with the barons to receive "The Articles of the Barons" which would specify which of the king's powers the barons wanted him to surrender in exchange for their continuing loyalty.

Langton, of course, knew exactly what was on the barons' "want list" because he'd helped scribe it. Once everyone was assembled at a mutually acceptable meeting place, it was Langton's intention to move back and forth between King John's advisors and the barons until a final agreement was reached that specified the rights of the barons and the rights of the king in great detail. There could be no peace, Langton knew, until everyone in the realm knew his place and his rights. As was inevitable in such cases, everything would already be pretty much agreed in advance, except the final wording. Langton had been working on it for months.

Whatever the final agreement turned out to be, it would almost certainly greatly weaken King John's power. On the other hand, it would also result in the barons re-pledging their oaths of loyalty to the king and agreeing to abandon London and Lincoln. Peace would be restored, at least temporarily, and the barons would be able to take their men and go home without paying any additional taxes.

Although the rebel barons didn't know it, the king had already decided to strip them of their lands and titles as soon as he rebuilt his support with aid of the Pope. He had seized some of their lands and castles prior to the battle of Bouvines, and, agreement or not, he intended to take the rest as soon as he was strong enough.

Under the circumstances, it wasn't enough for the king to make his mark and affix his seal on whatever was finally agreed. John had to show he was strong and unafraid of the rebel barons by doing it publically—the circumstances being that the king's supporters had been soundly defeated in

France the previous summer and that the emboldened barons and their French allies had already taken London and Lincoln.

King John had no choice. He had to show up to meet with the barons and accept their list of demands, and make an appearance of being strong when he did, otherwise the barons and their French allies would think he was weak and unable to withstand them. Then they would almost certainly reject Langton's proposed agreement and continue their plotting and attacks.

If the barons and the French attacked before he could rebuild his army, the king knew, the rebels were likely to take the rest of England and remove him from the throne before the Pope could come to his rescue by threatening to excommunicate the barons who were trying to get control of some of his divinely granted powers.

Using the archers based in Cornwall as the king's protectors during the king's initial meeting with the barons and the subsequent meeting to sign the agreement was suggested by Thomas, the Bishop of Cornwall, who was participating in the peace council. He'd thought of it when he heard gossiping courtiers tell each other that the king was trying to hire some of the foreign mercenaries who had fought against him in France.

It was a smart move on the part of the king; the arrival of the mercenaries' would help the king's rapidly dwindling royal supporters protect him from the barons, and make his forces appear stronger. On the other hand, however, in a manner comparable to throwing more wood on a fire, the king would have to levy new taxes on his barons to pay for them.

The commander of the king's army, Sir William Marshal, reluctantly confirmed to the king that the king's army needed the mercenaries or else it wouldn't have enough men to prevent the barons and their French supporters from attacking and killing him when John came out of Windsor Castle to meet with them.

Sir William and the king agreed enthusiastically, as you might well imagine, when Thomas, the Bishop of Cornwall, responded by suggesting an alternative to the foreign mercenaries—the archers of Cornwall, newly returned to England from the Holy Land after a successful raid on Algiers on their way home. The archers of Cornwall, Bishop Thomas suggested, could be contracted to protect the king instead of the foreign mercenaries who had so recently been fighting against him.

The king's enthusiasm for employing the archers grew rapidly when Thomas pointed out that the archers could be paid with the lands and holdings of the Earl of Devon, and those of any other of the rebel barons they killed, instead of with coins that would have to be raised with new taxes and partially paid in advance.

William Marshal was a wise man in addition to being a great knight who had won many tournaments and the loyal commander of the king's army; he knew that the king had no coins with which to pay mercenaries, and that the announcement of the new taxes needed to pay them would drive even more of the king's wavering supporters into the barons' camp. Accordingly he strongly advised the king to try to employ the fighting men of the company of archers based in Cornwall.

King John quickly agreed when he realized that using the lands and fiefs of the rebel barons to pay the archers meant he would not have to pay out any coins, coins he didn't have, and almost certainly could not get.

Employing the archers would be a good arrangement for everyone except the barons and the King of France *if* the men of the company of archers based in Cornwall were still in England, and *if* they made their marks on a contract, and *if* they actually came to Windsor to protect the king when he met with the barons.

If they agreed to help protect the king, William and his archers and sailors would then only be there to protect him because they were being paid, not because they supported King John or were enemies of the barons. The archers would remain neutral in the eyes of the barons and the church because everyone would understand that they were only there as hired mercenaries.

Mercenaries fighting for coins instead of causes was so much the custom of the times that some of the mercenaries the king had been trying to hire to help protect him from the barons and French had actually fought against him and his supporters at Bouvines the previous summer.

Things moved quickly once the possibility of employing the archers of Cornwall was suggested. King John offered William, the captain of the archers and

Thomas's younger brother, the Earl of Devon's lands if William would come to the meeting with a strong force of archers and sailors from Cornwall, three thousand men, and guard the king. Their presence would also be a "show of force" to the barons and their French allies—it would help deter the barons from attacking the king and his supporters by showing them that King John was not as weak and helpless as the barons and their French allies might think.

Thomas knew, of course, that the company of archers did not have anywhere near three thousand men in the whole world, let alone in England. But he claimed that it did because that was the number of mercenaries Sir William told the king he needed to hire to insure the king's safety.

Sir William and the king believed Thomas when he said Cornwall could provide three thousand men, in part because he was one of the Pope's bishops. He was, after all, the Bishop of Cornwall with a diocese he'd bought from the Pope some years earlier. Thomas had been able to buy the diocese and its bishopric cheap because Cornwall was extremely poor and always had been—so poor that it could support no priests or knights, its men had to work as sailors and archers to earn their bread, and even the Romans never bothered to build a road to it.

At least, that was the story of Cornwall's great poverty that Thomas and the company of archers based in Cornwall spread far and wide in an effort to be left alone by greedy churchmen and the king. In fact, the company of archers already had enough coins in Restormel Castle to pay the men of the company for the next two hundred and twenty-one years and almost one hundred war galleys and cogs—and more coins were arriving every month from selling prizes and carrying refugees, pilgrims, and cargos.

It worked; the men of Cornwall must be poor everyone agreed—or else they'd either be at court gossiping, and gambling, and seeking favours like everyone else, or plotting against the king in effort to get their taxes and scutages reduced.

Thomas's view of the situation was very much like that of his brother, William, the captain of the archers and more recently the Earl of Cornwall as a result of buying the virtually meaningless title from King John a few years earlier. William really didn't care what happened when the king met with the barons or who ended up being the king of England, so long as the winner left Cornwall and the company of archers he captained alone and untaxed.

The brothers' attitude toward the church and nobility were no surprise to those who knew them. They had been born serfs in an obscure farming village in Kent and had had enough experience with the church and nobility to know that they didn't want anyone else to hold the titles and attempt to use them to enrich themselves at the expense of Cornwall or, even more importantly, at the expense of the company of archers or their family.

Protecting Cornwall and the archers wasn't the only reason they'd bought their titles, of course—having them was helpful when they had to deal with people such as the Pope and the princes and lords who controlled the port cities where the company of archers earned its coins with galleys and transports carrying refugees and merchant cargos.

In any event, Thomas knew his brother would bring all his available archers to the meeting and protect King John if, and only if, he and his archers were adequately paid for their support, such as would be the case if they were to get the Earl of Devon's lands on the approaches to Cornwall and his seat at Rougemont Castle. Using their longbows, galleys, and bladed pikes was, after all, what the men of the company of archers did to earn their coins and bread.

Thomas had seen a draft of the charter Langton had scribed listing the specified liberties and rights of the king and his barons. He knew it would never work and he fully understood that the king would only agree to it in order to buy time in the hope that the barons would then disperse without fighting.

But Thomas also knew an opportunity when he saw one, and he proposed that King John sign a decree granting both Rougemont Castle and Devon's lands to the archers, and a "permanent and forever" exemption from taxes and scutages, in exchange for the archers protecting the king and providing a show of force when the king met with the barons.

King John agreed, and Thomas promptly scribed a parchment that gave the archers all that and more. The king quickly signed and sealed it, probably without even reading it, and hard riding couriers carried it and Thomas's parchment of explanation to William at Restormel Castle in Cornwall. That's where the company of archers had their training camp, the chests of coins no one knew they had, and Bishop Thomas's Latin-gobbling school.

It was a good thing for the king that he had agreed to hire the archers. Their presence, if they arrived in time, would tend to tip the balance of power back towards the king and, thus, make it much more likely an agreement could be reached and a civil war averted, at least temporarily.

Not that it would be a permanent agreement, Thomas knew. To the contrary, it was so fatally flawed that it would almost certainly sooner or later lead to war even if both sides signed it. The problem was that the agreement, the one that would be called the Magna Carta in the years ahead, was being drafted by the Archbishop of Canterbury, Stephen Langton—and required too much from King John and the Pope.

It was an interesting document. The latest draft of the agreement protected the rights of the church, limited the taxes the king could collect from his barons without their permission, and promised swift justice and protection from illegal imprisonment. These were acceptable to everyone, even the king and the Pope.

The big problem was that the agreement Langton drafted also included a fundamental change in the way England would be governed—it created a council of twenty-five barons to monitor the king's behaviour and authorized the council to override king's decisions by force if necessary. If put into effect, the agreement would effectively replace the king and his divine right to make laws and levy taxes with a collective of barons.

Thomas knew that neither King John nor the Pope would ever accept the king giving up his God-given right to govern and the coins it generated for him to share with the church, at least not for very long.

How long the resulting peace lasted after the king reached an agreement with the barons didn't matter so far as William and the archers were concerned. Once they fulfilled their contract with the king and took possession of Rougemont and its lands, they would never surrender them without a fight no matter who subsequently became king, even if it was the king himself who wanted them. But first they keep John alive long enough for him to meet with the barons and reach an agreement with them.

This is the story of how the archers of Cornwall affected the writing and signing of the Magna Carta just as the surviving participants told it some years later to the monks writing the history of the kingdom for those years.

—

Chapter One

Rougemont beckons.

I began reading the parchments I'd received from my priestly brother Thomas to those of my lieutenants who could be assembled to hear the news. As you might well imagine, I watched their eyes and faces closely as I read the parchments to them.

All five of my available lieutenants were sitting around me on the wooden benches that ran on both sides of the long wooden table in Restormel's hall and every man of them was listening intently—Raymond, Peter, Henry, Harold, and my son George.

Only two of my lieutenants were missing. Yoram was on Cyprus commanding our all-important citadel and shipping centre in the waters off the Holy Land, and my priestly brother Thomas was in Oxford attending the council William Marshal had hurriedly put together to advise the king how to deal with his rebel barons now that the rebels had seized both London and Lincoln.

I was reading Thomas's parchment to my lieutenants because, of them all, only my son George among my listeners knew how to read and scribe. He had been the second student my priestly brother had learnt to scribe and gobble Latin; I had been his first.

Or perhaps I should say I was reading the parchments from my brother Thomas to my "lieutenant commanders." We had finally decided, a few days earlier, after talking about it for several years, to change the names associated with the rank each of our men displayed on the front and back of his hooded Egyptian tunic.

The number of stripes I wore on the front and back of my tunic was still seven, but instead of being the captain of the Company of Archers, I was now, for better or worse, its "commander" or "commandant" instead of its captain, and the men who used to be my lieutenants were now my "lieutenant commanders" and still had six.

Below the lieutenant commanders were "majors" such as George with five stripes who used to be called "sergeant majors," and then the archers in command our individual cogs, galleys, and shipping posts who wore four stripes and used to be called "sergeant captains." Now they were to be simply called "captains."

We made the change because of the confusion that sometimes arose when an order came from me as the captain of all the men who'd made their marks on our company's roll as opposed to an order issued by one of the many archers who were the sergeant captains of our company's galleys, cogs, and shipping posts. We in the company of archers understood who was whom and that each our galleys was crewed by a company of almost one hundred archers, a galley company, to do its rowing and fighting, but some of the men with whom we dealt did not.

The biggest change was for the men who were our sergeants with three big stripes on the fronts and backs of their hooded tunics. We added a new rank, a new badge to show it, and a new name for the archers who held the rank.

It came about because one of our galleys lost its four-stripe sergeant captain in the middle of the recent fighting in Algiers harbour and his men got confused—they didn't know whose orders to follow because everyone trying to tell them what to do was a "sergeant" wearing three stripes.

In an effort to reduce the possibility of such confusion occurring again, the archer who was each galley's sergeant captain was now a "captain" and each galley captain's number two, the man who was to instantly take his place if he fell or was otherwise not available to make a decision, was now to be called his captain's "lieutenant" and wore a simple round badge above his three stripes to identify him as such.

A captain's lieutenant was the only man authorized to the captain's place and make all of his captain's decisions whenever his captain was unavailable to make them himself. After that it would be the sergeants in order of their seniority, and then the chosen men.

Not much else was changed except the names. I still had my scarred face and wore my rusty chain shirt under my tunic whenever I went outside of Restormel's walls, and I always wore a hidden "surprise knife" hidden under my tunic on each of my wrists. So did Thomas and George and some of the other men, wear chain shirts, I mean.

Thomas and George also wore surprise knives. Wearing hidden wrist knives was a family tradition started by Thomas when he was a lad due to some problems he had with several of the older monks at the monastery, and it was a good thing he did; they had saved our lives on several occasions.

Having new names for many of our ranks was all a bit confusing at first, but Henry and Harold said it had to be done and Thomas had agreed; so we did it. The new names will take some time getting used to, at least for me, after all these years of thinking of myself as a captain.

****** *William*

"Well, that's it," I said when I finished reading Thomas's message to my five lieutenant commanders and one available major, and began scratching one of Helen's rat-catching cats under the chin. "What do you think?"

"I like it," Henry responded enthusiastically before anyone else had a chance to even open his mouth.

Fast off the mark was our Henry. That's why he commanded all of our foot archers when they were on land and was responsible for them being learnt to do such things as push arrows out of a longbow, and how to fight together and walk on the same foot whilst they were marching.

"Ever since we got here we've been talking about how to get rid of that damn Devon so he'd stop trying to take Cornwall away from us. So let's settle things once and forever by killing Devon and taking Rougemont—and then keeping a strong force of archers in the castle to hold it so the king can't replace Devon with someone who might try to take Cornwall from us.

"Besides, if we get rid of Devon we can settle some of our older archers and wounded men on his lands. It would improve our food supplies and each of his seven knightly fiefs would do nicely for five or six of our older men and invalids who are daft enough to want to retire and go on half pay here in Cornwall despite the weather."

It was vintage Henry, of course. He had been talking about retiring for years and had even built a fine two room hovel with a fireplace on Cyprus for himself and his dear wife whom he'd met when she was spying for us in Constantinople.

Henry would never do it, of course, retire I mean, because he loved being a commander in a fine fight and counting his coins. But he liked to talk about Cyprus's warm weather whenever Cornwall was cold or he was at sea and it was wet and miserable—and he enjoyed spending winters with our archers on Cyprus as much as I did.

There was total agreement with Henry's thoughts from everyone around the table, including me. Little wonder in that; going for Rougemont and the Earl of Devon and his lands was a move we'd been talking about ever since we landed in Cornwall years ago and had to kill some of the earl's relatives when they attacked poor old Lord Edmund's widow in an effort to get their hands on her keep and lands at Bossiney.

Besides, we'd been back in Cornwall for almost a month following our raid on Algiers on our way back here from wintering on Cyprus and we were all getting bored, I least I know I was. Let's face it, spending time making sure our new apprentices were properly learnt so they'd know how to push arrows out of a longbow and walk together on the same foot and set their stakes and hold their bladed pikes was necessary and had to be done; but it got old and boring very fast.

"But do we go to Rougemont first and carve up the Earl of Devon like a Christmas goose, which is what I think we should do; or do we go straight to London to support the king and take Rougemont on our way back home?" Peter asked. "And how long will it take us to assemble enough archers to do it?"

There were no flies on Peter London. That's why the son of a London alehouse woman was my number two even though he was a bit younger than my other lieutenants.

Peter looked at Harold and Henry as he asked his questions, and rightly so. Harold was in charge of our cogs and other transports, war galleys, and our men when they were on them just as Henry was in charge of our men when they were on land. Harold would know, if anyone would, where each of our transports and cogs was located at the moment and how many of our fighting men it had on board; Henry would know how many archers we already had in Cornwall and how many more, if any, were available for us to quickly bring in from elsewhere.

"We took a chance on the weather and came back early this year at the end of the storm season so we could hit the Algerians while their galleys were still mostly beached without their crews on board. It worked and we brought some of the prizes we took to London to sell when we came back to spend the summer in England. So we've got almost a thousand experienced archers here in Cornwall," Henry said as Harold and everyone around the table, including me, nodded his agreement. Then he continued.

"And then, of course, we've got Raymond's entire company of horse archers and outriders at Okehampton guarding the border, and about three hundred apprentices in training ranging from those ready to put their first stripe on their tunics to those who are goddamn useless and should never be allowed to make their marks on our roll. Plus, we've got the experienced archers we kept in Cornwall to sergeant and put the learning on the apprentices.

All in all, those men, and two or three hundred sailors and volunteers to carry water and such, would give us enough men to look like three thousand if we move them around a lot. The king won't be counting will he?"

"Besides," Peter broke in with a satisfied grin. "One of our archers with a longbow and a hooked and bladed pike is worth four or five of their knights and soldiers, even if the king and the barons don't know it yet."

Peter was my second in command. He was from London and always liked a good fight with enemies who looked down on us because we weren't knights.

"Aye, our lads are certainly better, much better, because of their modern weapons and constant training," I responded with a caution in my voice as I leaned forward and looked sternly around the table.

"But we don't want anyone to find out how effective our longbows and bladed pikes are, or how we've learnt our men use them, do we? If the king and the gentry ever find out, they might start training archers and begin fighting the way we do. There are rumours that William Marshal put together a company of Norman archers for the king to use in France last year. Fortunately for us, the poor sods were lost at Bouvines because the king appointed a captain who didn't know how to employ them properly."

Then my dear Helen brought us another skin of fresh ale and we settled down to make our plans.

We quickly agreed that taking Rougemont Castle and Exeter from the Earl of Devon was much more important to us than temporarily making King John feel safe and look powerful; so we decided to read the king's contract to our advantage and go straight to Exeter to take Rougemont Castle and put paid to the long account of troubles the Earl of Devon had run up with us.

"The king isn't likely to complain and get angry with us so long as we are fighting his enemies," I said. "And if he does, we can tell him that we had to bottle up Devon and his men in Exeter so they wouldn't be able to join up with the other barons and attack him. Besides, once we start fighting with Devon it will be too late for the king to change his mind and try to call us off."

We also agreed that there was little chance the French or the earl's fellow rebel barons would come all the way to Exeter and attempt to relieve Devon if we brought him to battle or laid a siege on his hold at Rougemont. They were, we thought, all focused on London and replacing the king and, besides, Exeter was too far away and trying to relieve it would take them too long because they'd have to march all the way to Exeter and all the way back.

Anyway, that's what we all hoped and told each other; so we convinced ourselves it was true and decided to march against Devon before we marched to join the loyalists supporting the king.

In any event, the decision was made and it seemed a good time to proceed—our captains and the local fishermen were reporting the coast to be clear of French sails at this end of the Channel. It was now or never; once we started marching for Exeter, we knew we'd either be taking Rougemont and Devonshire or go down trying.

****** *William*

We assembled all of the available archers, weapons, and supplies, loaded our wains and horse carts, and, three days later as soon as the sun came over the horizon and began moving overhead, just over nineteen hundred men, eighteen galley companies of archers and their auxiliaries, started marching for Exeter to the beat of each galley company's rowing drum.

It was a grand scene with more snivelling women and children running about than I would have thought possible. Helen and Tori had presented me with a new tunic, trimmed my beard, and picked my lice most nicely the night before, and did other things to please me as well.

Thomas's assistant, Angelo Priestly, was there with all twenty-two of the students in Thomas's school to see us off. They were all bright eyed and excited, and trying very hard not to show it. Several of the school's older boys had been promoted to apprentice sergeants and allowed to make their marks on the company roll to join us scribes and aides. Thomas would gobble the church words at them and wave his cross to make them priests when they got to Windsor.

Our plans were simple, as all good plans must be until they have to be changed when the fighting starts and the realities set in. After we take Rougemont and Exeter we would split up and half of the foot archers and all the horse archers would march on to London; the other half of the foot archers would return to Restormel and row for London in our galleys.

Using two different routes would make more likely that at least some of our men would reach London in time to accompany the king to his meeting and appear to fulfil our contract. As was our custom, no women or merchants would accompany us. We would be a war army with nothing to distract us or slow us down.

Our initial plan was for our entire force to wade across the River Tamar at the Launceston ford, join up with Raymond's horse archers at Okehampton, and march south down the London Road to Devon's Rougemont Castle on the outskirts of Exeter—and kill the rotten bastard who held it.

It was a reasonable plan and the decision to march along that route wasn't a difficult decision to make; it would be by far the fastest way for us to get to Exeter, even if it meant we'd have quite a bit farther to march than if we tried to walk straight to Rougemont from Restormel.

In fact, even though the route we would be marching might take us a much greater distance, it would be much faster because we could use the existing roads, cart paths, and river fords. Attempting to go from here straight to Exeter by traveling across the infrequent farmlands, streams, and the impassable, thick forests of western Devon was a fool's game. Only a bird could do that.

******

Three days of dawn to dusk marching was all that it took for us to reach Okehampton, the first leg on our long march that would, if all went well, end up with all of our available archers joining the king's forces near Windsor. We made good time because it didn't rain all that much and the road was clear.

For me, traveling the road to Okehampton brought back many good memories. I was looking forward to visiting the castle once again even though Isabel Courtenay was no longer there to welcome me into her bed. She had married last year and gone to her new husband.

And getting my feet wet at the Launceston ford reminded me that we needed to repair the bridge over the Fowey.

It was while I was bouncing up and down on my horse, and trying to distract myself from my sore arse, that I began to think once again about taking the name of Courtenay for myself and my family.

No one would really mind, I decided. The name was vacant because the original Courtenay of Okehampton was long dead of being stuck with arrows while attacking us, and Isabel was no longer a Courtenay as a result of being married to a new husband and her son becoming her husband's heir and adopting his name. At least, that's what Raymond said his wife told him.

Thomas had been saying for years that our family needed a family name to better identify ourselves. I think I decided at long last to do it, take a family name that is, because I wanted to put my past behind me.

Besides, times were changing and using only the Christian name me mum gave me no longer seemed proper—because in these modern days only serfs and kings used one name. I certainly wasn't a king and never would be, and I was so long gone from the village and being a serf that I could barely remember how bad it had been before my mum died of the sweating pox and Thomas left the monastery to rescue me and take me crusading with King Richard as one of his archers.

I had thought about using captain as my family name and making myself known to everyone as William Captain. But the idea that my children would all then be known as the Captains didn't sound right either. My son George, for example, would then be Major George Captain which could cause confusion and somehow didn't roll off my tongue quite right.

Archer would have been a fine name for me to use except so many of our men were already using it on the company roll that it too might cause confusion. Courtenay sounded better, a bit more like we were one of the old Norman families instead of what we really were—commoners who got lucky and escaped the clutches of their owners and the church.

Besides, the Courtenay name was available and associated with one of our keeps. Truth be told, I liked the way it sounded.

In any event, it was while I was bouncing along on my way to a war against the Earl of Devon with a sore arse that, to distract myself from the pain, I once again thought about naming myself as William Courtenay of Okehampton.

I could, I finally decided, tie myself to the name all nice and tidy by claiming to have inherited Okehampton as a distant cousin of Isabel's late husband, the Courtenay lord of Okehampton who we'd killed *before* she married him. That was at the same time we "bought" Okehampton from Courtenay by forging his mark on the sale parchment and placing it and the required notice of sale in the local church records.

My final decision was made while I sat on my horse and watched the galley companies of archers march past to the beat of their rowing drums. From now on I would use two names and there was no one to say they weren't mine all right and proper.

It didn't entirely work, though; my arse was still sore.

****** *William*

Okehampton Castle standing against the sky was a grand sight when I once again glimpsed it through the trees. It's truly splendid and defensible keep and had been the home of the company's horse archers ever since we took it off Courtenay.

Our welcome was warm when we rode across its two drawbridges, and dismounted in its inner bailey. Raymond had ridden on ahead with his horse archers, and had food, drink, and shelter waiting for us. He and his wife Wanda knew what to do; it was not the first time an army of the company's archers had passed over Okehampton's drawbridges to spend the night on its way to a battle or coming home from one. It began to rain just as we arrived.

The rain was still coming down as Wanda, Raymond's wife from the land beyond the deserts of the Holy Land, lit two beeswax candles in one of the two rooms above castle's the great hall so we could see enough to eat and drink.

One of the rooms was where Raymond and his wife lived; the other room was the room where the lieutenant commanders and majors and I would sup and drink ale and talk this evening, and afterwards we would sleep. Our apprentice sergeants would be with us to run our errands and scribe for us and, hopefully, begin to learn how to be captains.

Our young apprentice sergeants from Thomas's school walked up the stone stairs to our room with us to silently listen and learn. We left our four-stripe captains and their three stripe lieutenants and sergeants to pack themselves into the great hall below us for their eating and sleeping.

The rest of the archers stayed outside the keep; they overfilled the tower rooms in the castle's walls, its stables, and some hastily erected tents in both the inner and outer baileys. The sharp and pungent smell of horse piss and men who never washed was everywhere.

But at least they watered their arses after they shite and sometimes washed their tunics, unlike the Templars who always smelled bad because they didn't wipe their arses because they were trying to live like Jesus who was a god and didn't need to do the things a human man would do.

The room was familiar to me, and being in it once again brought back memories. I knew quite well the stone walls where we were eating and drinking, and all of us would be sleeping that night to stay out of the rain; Isabel and her maid used to live in it, and I had visited her here more than once.

Somehow the room looked different, and then I realized what had changed—Isabela had taken her sitting stools with her, and the woven carpets from the Saracen lands that used to cover some of the floor were gone. Only the old wooden table remained with all its scars and stains.

******

We were already seated on the table's benches and beginning to fill our bowls from the ale bucket when Raymond came in with an excited look on his face and hurried towards me at the far end of the table.

Henry and Harold saw his excitement and quickly scooted down to make room for him to sit down next to me. He did have important news: Several of his outriders, he told me as my lieutenants listened intently, had just ridden in with an important report about the Earl of Devon.

As soon as Raymond began telling us about the outriders' report, I knew he was right to be excited and got rather excited myself, and so did everyone else. His outriders had brought in a report that seemed to be good news, very good news.

The report had come from the young four-striper, the one-time apprentice sergeant and school friend of George's who was now a four-stripe captain commanding Raymond's outriders. He and most of his men had been sent by Raymond to watch the Exeter Road from a temporary hillside camp located in the forest north of the city.

George sat up and leaned forward with great interest as soon as Raymond began speaking—both because of what he was hearing and because Richard, the young man Raymond was talking about, was a friend of his from Thomas's school in the wooden shed running along the north side of Restormel's inner curtain wall. They had fought together and played a big role in defeating the Earl of Devon when the earl and an army of his supporters tried to invade Cornwall a few years earlier.

I immediately recognized the name of the outrider captain who had sent the messenger. I knew who he was and could picture him behind my eyes as soon as Raymond began talking about him and what he had seen.

His name was Richard and he had been Raymond's apprentice sergeant and scribe several years ago when Devon and some of his supporters tried to invade Cornwall. Richard had done so well in the fighting and thinking behind his eyes that Raymond had kept him at Okehampton and given him command of all of his outriders after Devon's army had been destroyed.

For some strange reason as Raymond spoke, I wondered if Richard knew he was now a captain because of our name changes instead of a sergeant. It didn't matter, of course; either way he had four stripes and the same command. But I wondered if he knew and it bothered me most strange that it did.

Richard's important information was that two days ago he and his outriders had seen four groups of men led by knights hurrying down the road towards Exeter carrying spears and long-handled farm tools such as hoes and scythes that the village levies often used as weapons. That had been followed by the number of wains and men on the road becoming less frequent than usual in the days that followed.

Uncertain as to what it might mean, Richard himself had walked down from the watchers' camp to sit alone and unarmed by the side of the road. There he had chatted up the local serfs and slaves as they walked to and from their fields, particularly when they stopped to cup their hands and drink some water from the little stream of clear water that crossed the road nearby.

The people he met and talked to were almost all women, and most of them were happy to talk to the cheerful young man who was resting there; they confirmed that Devon's knights and the men of his village levies and their weapons, such as they were, had been summoned to Rougemont Castle by the earl.

What it almost certainly meant, according to the message from Richard, was that the Earl of Devon had called in his knights and village levies and was forming up his army to join the rebel barons assembling to meet with the king. What it also meant, since Richard hadn't seen any armed men coming the other way, was that Devon and his army were still at Rougemont.

We appeared to have gotten to Okehampton and the only road from Exeter to London in time to intercept them—if they were coming.

"So what should we do?" I asked my lieutenants.

I knew the answer, of course, but the courtesies had to be observed.

Chapter Two

We march south and don't get very far.

There was no question at all as to what my lieutenants and I would have preferred to do in response to Devon gathering his forces. Ideally, we would stay near Launceston and wait for Devon and his army to come to us when they marched to join the barons who were assembling their forces near Windsor. That way we could both fight them on ground of our choosing and have a supply base and a hospital where we could barber and bleed our sick and wounded.

Unfortunately, we all agreed, that choice was not available to us—we couldn't wait; we had to come to grips with Devon quickly and get on our way to join the king at Windsor as soon as possible. We had no choice; we'd begin marching south toward Exeter as soon as the sun arrived in the morning.

But then my son George raised a question.

"Is it possible Devon has spies in our camp or the king's just as we have spies in his? Perhaps he received word of our contract with King John and summoned his men to help fight us off because he knows we're coming to attack him at Rougemont Castle?"

Everyone looked at everyone else and nothing was said until Henry snorted in disdain, leaned forward with a great wave of his hand, and set us straight as he swung his leg over the bench and stood up to leave.

"It don't matter, do it? We've got to march down there and kill him and his heirs whether he's getting ready to fight us or not—so let's make sure our men will be eating all proper-like in the morning and get enough sleep; we've got a busy day coming. I want to have the men fed and on the road marching south by the time the sun gets to us."

****** *George*

We all slept together in the same room where we supped. I was roused from my sleep while it was still dark and my dingle must have been thinking about bedding Beth and Becky.

I promptly banged my knee against one of the benches next to the table where we'd supped last night, drew a curse when I stepped on the hand of someone who had been sleeping under the table, and stumbled my way to the stairs clutching my longbow, quivers, and my hooded rain skin.

All around me cursing and muttering men were getting to their feet. The only light in the dimly lit room was from a single candle lantern someone must have lit. I was hungry, needed to piss in the worst way, and my neck hurt most sorely from sleeping on the hard stone floor even though I had folded up my rain skin and used it for a pillow under my head.

There was no doubt about it; I was excited and ready for the sun to arrive on its daily trip around the world so we could get started.

My apprentice, Thomas, whom the archers have already started to name as Thomas Young to distinguish him from all the other archers named Thomas including my uncle, had been next to me and had gotten to his feet at the same time I did; but I soon lost him in the darkness and the confusion of having so many men around me and my jumping away when I stepped on someone's hand and almost had my legs pulled out from under me.

I didn't see or hear my father or any of his lieutenants. They had put their heads down to sleep next to the stairs and must have already made their way out of the crowded room.

Things moved quickly after I stumbled half asleep down the narrow and winding stone stairs and through the crowded great hall to the door to the bailey. I followed the crowd of grumbling and foul-mouthed men until I found a place to piss. Then I grabbed some cold flatbreads and pieces of cheese from a great pile in the middle of the bailey and stood in line for a bowl of morning ale to swish through my teeth and settle my thirst.

Someone had stayed up all night cooking the bread and cutting up the cheeses, that's for sure; probably some of the castle's servants from the local village.

I went in search of my horse with my hands and mouth full of bread and cheese and with even more tucked safely inside my tunic to eat later. It took some time to find my brown ambler gelding because all the men in the horse archers' unlit stables were engaged in the same chore in the darkness. But I finally did.

And that's where I found Thomas, my missing apprentice. We had gotten separated when we woke up because of the darkness. That I might leave without him had so worried Thomas, he later confessed, that he had come straight to our horses as soon as he made his way out of the keep.

He was a smart lad, young Thomas; he knew that sooner or later I'd show up to get my horse. He had been worried, he explained, that I would mount up and ride off without him. And, of course, being a newbie, he hadn't stopped to get any bread and cheese. So I shared some of mine with him.

Like all the other long-serving veterans, I had taken all the food I could carry so I'd have something to eat later. He'd soon learn to do the same; maybe he just did. In any event, Thomas was most grateful for having something to eat and apologized so many times that I grumped and told him to stop.

****** *George*

Thomas Young and I were riding south in the middle of the column of horse archers on the road to Exeter by the time the sun arrived the next morning. Each of the horse archers was leading his supply horse with his extra food and arrows and the bladed pike he used when he fought on foot. Many of them were eating some of the extra bread and cheese they had wisely grabbed off the morning pile.

The walking archers with their wains and horse carts were marching about three miles behind us and undoubtedly doing the very same thing. Sometimes when the wind changed we could hear their marching drums and their shouted songs and chants over the sound of our talking and the clatter of our horses' hooves.

It was good day for a march; it wasn't raining, the sun was out, and the spirits of the archers riding their horses and leading their supply horses were high all around me. I was riding in the middle of the horse archers in order to talk and reminisce with old friends I'd served with when the army of the Earl of Devon and his friends from among the eastern and northern lords tried to invade Cornwall a few years ago, and I had been a sergeant with the horse archers when they and their outriders destroyed it.

As you might imagine, we reminisced and told stories to each other about what we'd done, and some of them were even true. Thomas and the other young archers who'd just put on their first stripe and never had been to war listened to our tales and banter and were greatly impressed.

All in all, it was fine day to be alive. As we rode south along the old Roman road the archers teased each other and remembered to each other what they'd done and seen and the stories and tall tales they'd heard. Whenever the road ahead of me bent, I could periodically see my father and a couple of his lieutenants riding at the very front of the column. They too seemed to be enjoying themselves and telling each other stories and laughing and waving their hands about as they rode.

It seems strange to tell, but I was happy to be an archer going to war. Truth be told, the men I was with seemed to be more family to me than even Beth and Becky and our little ones.

The men riding around me seemed to be content as well. None of them appeared to be worrying about losing his life or suffering a painful injury in the battles that were coming. To the contrary, as I had long ago observed, real fighting men, such as those riding all about me on the road, seemed to put such thoughts out of their minds and were pleased and content when their sergeants and captains were satisfied with how things were going.

It was really quite strange when you think about it; we were going to war and might well be killed or terribly hurt at any moment, and yet the archers riding around me were smiling and telling jokes to each other as if we were in a wedding party taking an anxious groom to his new wife. Their high spirits were catching and I soon found myself laughing at their ribald jokes and smiling in agreement at their cheerful comments and stories, and adding my own.

We had reached the Exeter road three or four hours earlier and were making good time riding towards the south with Uncle Raymond's horse archers leading the way and a long column of marching archers strung out along the road starting about three miles behind us.

Uncle Raymond was an uncle because all of the handful of archers who had followed my father over Edmund's wall with me in his arms when I was a wee boy had helped raise and protect me and had been my uncles for as long as I could remember. I was part of their family and they were part of mine; they were my uncles and had been for all of my life.

******

We were riding along happily without a care in the world when everything changed. It happened a couple of hours after the sun passed over the puffy white clouds above us and began heading west as part of its daily circle around the world.

My father and his lieutenant commanders and their apprentice sergeants were visible riding at the front of Uncle Raymond's main body of horse archers when some of the men around me began standing up on their stirrups to look and point down the road far beyond the front of our column. Then everyone stood up in their stirrups and began talking and pointing at the same time.

Little wonder in that; the road bent a little up ahead and we could see two riders in the distance coming towards us—and they were flogging their horses and riding hard in an effort to reach us. Each of them was leading a remount.

Within the space of a few heartbeats we were all standing in our saddles with a hand cupped over our eyes to help us see the rapidly approaching horsemen. Some of the men behind us kicked their horses in the ribs and moved off the road so they could see more clearly—until their sergeants began shouting at them to return to their ranks.

Less than a minute later we could see the tunics of the two distant riders and knew they were a couple of our own horse archers leading their supply horses; almost certainly they were either some of the men Uncle Raymond had riding far out in front of our column to prevent an ambush, or perhaps the horses being led were remounts and they were a couple of Richard's outriders coming in with something important to report.

Almost immediately, to our further surprise and with everyone around me doing much more pointing and loudly talking with excited voices, we could see more riders in the distance and they were riding hard as well. There were three of them and at least one of them was leading a string of horses.

From where we were, we couldn't tell if the second group of riders were pursuing our men or were more of our own men who were returning to our army for some reason.

All around me on the road, the horse archers instinctively came to a halt even before Uncle Raymond raised his arm and the sergeants began repeating the order for everyone to pull up. A couple of horse archers riding ahead of me began stringing their longbows even though no order had yet been given.

Their act of stringing their bows spread down our column of riders like a wave washing through a harbour that rocks every anchored boat. Suddenly everywhere along our column bows were being strung and quivers adjusted. Even my apprentice sergeant, young Thomas, caught their excitement and began stringing his bow.

I was the only one around me who didn't—I could see my father and Uncle Raymond standing on their stirrups to better see what was coming. They didn't seem alarmed; they appeared to be more curious than anything else.

Something was happening and those of us riding in the middle of the column of horse archers didn't have the slightest idea of what it might be. Well, we'd know soon enough, wouldn't we? And that's when it finally dawned on me that I was a major with five stripes and should have been riding with my father and his lieutenants at the head of the column, not back here larking and talking with the men.

****** *George*

"Silence in the ranks," shouted an irate Uncle Raymond over his shoulder as he and my father and his other lieutenants began riding forward to meet the oncoming riders who were now quite clearly two of ours. The sergeants loudly repeated the "Silence" order as I ambled slowly forward along the edge of the stopped column with my apprentice sergeant, Thomas Young, following along behind me.

I wanted to find out what was happening and, truth be told, I felt more than a little guilty. I should have been up front with my father and his lieutenants instead of riding in the middle of the column talking with the men I knew from the days when I'd led some of them in an earlier war.

What the hell is going on here?

The first two of the incoming riders, both two-stripe chosen men, obviously long-serving veterans, reined in and knuckled their foreheads to salute as they began their report. They were clearly tired and out of breath, and their horses were exhausted and blowing hard. I knew immediately that they were outriders because they were leading remounts with saddles, not supply horses. They were pointing down the road and talking rapidly.

My father and his lieutenants immediately began having what appeared to be an urgent conversation with them and with each other. I could tell from their expressions and gestures. But I couldn't hear what was being said so I decided to continue riding forward and try to listen.

I hadn't gotten close enough to hear everything that was being said when, suddenly, Uncle Raymond shouted an order for a sergeant by the name of Rufe to bring his men and follow him. Then, without waiting for an answer, Uncle Raymond wheeled his horse around and started galloping down the road towards the three oncoming riders.

A couple of heart beats later, as I reached my father and his lieutenants at the front of the column, two files of horse archers, obviously Rufe and his men, came charging out of the column behind me and streamed past us on both sides without their supply horses.

I saw their faces as they thundered by—they were excited and they obviously didn't have a clue as to why they were galloping down the road behind their commander. Those of them who had not already done so had dropped their reins and were stringing their bows as they galloped past us.

Almost at the same moment, my father's young apprentice sergeant, John Small, wheeled his horse around and began kicking it in the ribs and whipping it with his reins while he galloped back along the column of horse archers strung out behind us. He too had an excited look on his face; and he was riding so badly that I was afraid he would fall off.

It was obvious to everyone that he was carrying an important order to the men marching on foot about three miles behind us; our horses were never whipped or beaten unless there was an absolutely urgent need for speed or distance. They were all amblers and much too valuable for that.

We sat on our horses and watched as Uncle Raymond closed on the three remaining riders ahead of us on the road, stopped for a brief moment to exchange words with them as Rufe and his men galloped up behind him, and then kicked his horse in the ribs and gave a great winding "follow me" motion with his arm to continue leading Rufe and his dozen or so men on down the road at a gallop.

Before Uncle Raymond and his men passed out of sight, they turned off the road and I saw them switch from galloping their horses to what I knew to be the fast amble that our horses could maintain for hours if necessary. Uncle Raymond was on the move and in a hurry.

I reached my father's side a few seconds later. He had pulled his horse to a halt and had dismounted. He was waiting with Henry and Peter for the arrival of the second group of riders. The first two outriders had already dismounted and were starting to walk their badly winded horses to help them recover.

It was about then that I realized that one of the three hard-riding men approaching us was sorely wounded and that his labouring horse was being led by one of the other men— and that man was my friend, and fellow student in Uncle Thomas's school years earlier, Richard, the captain of our outriders. The third man coming in behind them was leading a string of remounts; he too was an outrider.

Something important had happened or was taking place, and I didn't have the slightest clue as to what it might be.

****** *George*

Nothing happened for a few minutes after Richard and his wounded man reached us except a lot of talking and arm waving by Richard as I watched and listened as best I could. The gist of Richard's message, at least so far as I was able to hear it, was that Devon and his army were on the road about a two hour march to the south and slowly coming this way. There were, Richard reported, perhaps five or six hundred men on foot and forty or fifty men on horseback, almost certainly knights and their armour-wearing squires and sergeants.

The good news, according to Richard, was that Devon was behaving as if he didn't know we were coming south towards him just as he, Richard, hadn't known we were coming until he saw the horse archers spread out and riding well ahead of the column. Richard had immediately recognized them for what they were—horse archers sent ahead to look for ambushes and danger. The Earl of Devon, he said, to the obvious delight of my father and his lieutenants, felt secure riding on his own lands; he didn't have any watchers riding out in front of his army.

The wounded archer, it seemed, had not been wounded in such a way as to alert Devon that we might be coming; he'd taken a nasty sword slice in his side yesterday from a courier Richard's men had stopped and searched without finding anything of significance. The courier's message, whatever it was, had died with him and they'd hidden his body.

Richard was just beginning to explain why he'd brought the wounded man in with him when I noticed the foot archers marching a couple of miles behind us had turned around and appeared to be double timing back up the road in the opposite direction. I raised my eyebrows and lifted my hand in a questioning gesture towards my father when I saw them go. Henry saw me do it and answered my unspoken question.

"We passed through a much better place for us to fight a couple of hours ago," Henry said as his excited horse raised its head and began skittering about, "where they won't see us until it's too late because the forest is so thick and the trees come right down to the road."

Henry didn't have a chance to say more. My father raised his arm and signalled for the column of riders to follow him—and began leading the column of horse archers away from the road to our left at a steady, distance-eating amble. A handful of women working in the fields saw us go. But they were the only ones who did. The fields were mostly empty of all but sheep and the few travellers we'd seen had melted away by running into the distant fields and trees at the first sight of our men.

The travellers on the road had no idea who we might have been, of course, but no traveller in his right mind wanted to encounter a large group of armed men on England's roads these days; at least, not outside of Cornwall.

I put my heels to my horse in order to catch up with my father. As I did, Henry and Peter pulled their horses around and they and their apprentice sergeants began galloping down the road. I had heard my father give them their orders. They were going to take command of our eighteen galley companies of foot archers—and prepare them to ambush the Earl of Devon's army.

Richard rode next to me as we chased after my father. My friend Richard had already changed horses with a young horse archer and was riding next to me on his relatively fresh new horse; the horse archer whose horse he had taken had already mounted his supply horse and begun slowly leading the wounded man and Richard's spent horse towards the retreating foot archers and on to Okehampton for rest and barbering.

"Richard," I shouted as I motioned for him to ride next to me, "what happened?"

****** *George*

It was a long and interesting story. I got most of it as Richard and I rode together and talked for about half an hour until the road was almost out of sight behind us. It wasn't until we talked about what would happen during and after we met Devon's army that the enormity of what we were going to try to do finally struck me.

A few minutes later my father pulled up his horse, motioned for the two of us to join him, and shouted out an order to Uncle Raymond's major and the rest of the horse archers to keep going.

"You two are to remain here. I want you to stay out of sight and watch the road. Just watch, that's all you are to do. Don't show yourself unless it's absolutely necessary even if you see outriders or some of our watchers coming in. You're to stay out of sight, and then come tell me what you've seen after you watch Devon and his entire column of men pass on the road and counted them.

I'll be waiting behind that hill over there with the horse archers. After Devon and his men pass, we're going to ride in behind them to cut off anyone who escapes from the foot archers."

He grinned as he pointed to a small, nearby hill towards the side of which the horse archers were riding, and added more to his explanation.

"The foot archers under Peter and Henry are going to ambush Devon and his men in the middle of the thick wood we passed through two or three hours ago. Devon's survivors, if there are any, will probably run this way in an effort to get back to Rougemont. We'll hide behind the hill until they pass and then ride back to the road and position ourselves to cut them off. We'll move out to do so when you come back to get us."

****

Richard and I dismounted behind a stand of trees and walked back about a couple of hundred paces to where we could see the road without being seen. We took our longbows and quivers with us. Thomas, my apprentice sergeant, remained with our horses with orders to let them rest and eat grass, but to leave them properly saddled and ready to be brought forward to us and ridden on a moment's notice.

We each sat down with our back against a tree and commenced watching. Several times we saw groups people pass in front of us on the road, almost all were women and many of them had young children with them. They were obviously walking back to their hovels after a day of working in the fields. There were also periodic travellers on the road.

What quickly caught our eye was that all of them were walking north away from Exeter. We never saw a single traveller heading south. They were probably being held by the foot archers to prevent them from warning Devon's army that we were waiting for them.

"Look; here they come." Richard's call woke me from my brief nap with a snort. I went from a drowsy nap to wide awake in one heartbeat as I rolled over on my side to look.

Sure enough, in the distance to my left a straggling mass of men was beginning to come into sight on the road. Some were riding but most were walking. What surprised us both was that they were moving north on the road from Exeter without any sort of organization or anyone riding out in front watching for danger.

Scattered amongst them were wains and horse carts and a number of women and pedlars. A few of the women were carrying or leading small children. The pedlars had their own horse-drawn carts and wains.

Richard and I had already gathered the necessary counting stones as we'd been learnt at school. We each began moving a stone into a new pile for every ten walkers who might be soldiers and another stone into another new pile for every rider we saw and for every horse being led that looked as though it might belong to a dismounted rider who was walking.

They were moving so slowly that it took them the better part of an hour to straggle past us. Some were clearly mounted knights and once we saw what looked like a banner being carried on a lance in the middle of a group of half a dozen or so riders.

It was, Richard and I assured each other several times, almost certainly the Earl of Devon and his knights and their village levies. Who else could it be except the earl's army?

"They couldn't be French, could they?"

******

Richard and I each had two large piles of stones by the time the tail of Devon's army began passing in front of us. We counted the stones in our piles as we waited for the tail end of his army to finish moving far enough out of sight, so we could return unseen to our horses.

There were, we agreed when we finished counting and compared our counts, just over six hundred men, almost certainly Devon's village levies, plus either forty two or forty seven horses that were being ridden or could be ridden by knights and men at arms who were walking for some reason.

Most of the riders were not wearing their armour; it was apparently being carried on the wains and carts or tied on to the supply horses walking behind some of them. There were also forty or fifty women including some with children and a number of merchant wains. It was the typical army of an English baron marching to war.

"A dozen of my outriders could do for that entire lot," Richard muttered with both disgust and pride in his voice as the last of them passed out of sight and we climbed to our feet.

"Aye," I agreed as we crouched low and began walking back to our horses. "And unless God grants them a miracle, there won't be many of them coming back this way for the horse archers to catch. Poor sods."

Richard and I mounted our horses and rode back to my father and the horse archers to report what we'd seen. They were easy to find on the other side of the little hill near a little stream—it's hard to miss several hundred horse archers and their supply horses.

Uncle Raymond was coming in with the rest of Richard's outriders as we arrived. He'd gone to fetch Richard's outriders to join us, and to see for himself what kind of army we'd be going up against and where they were on the road. Richard was as elated to see his men as they were to see him and learn that their wounded friend had been saved and would get proper barbering at Okehampton.

Chapter Three

Devon's army.

Commander William sent me galloping back to take command of the column of foot archers and prepare an ambush on Devon's army where the road to London goes through a thick forest. Henry came with me to be my second. We hurried because we didn't know how much time we would need to get the foot archers into position.

Henry and I, with our apprentice sergeants gamely riding to keep up with us, caught up with the last of the foot archers long before the London road began to enter the thick woods. Only a few of the double-timing archers had dropped out from their efforts and were walking slowly along the road, but they were all clearly getting tired and beginning to falter. At Henry's immediate suggestion, I ordered the galley captains and the men of their companies to resume walking as we caught up to the rear of the column and began riding rapidly along the companies of labouring men.

"Peter," Henry shouted over to me as we hurried along past the column and entered the woods with our apprentice sergeants riding behind us. "I think there is an open area about a mile or so ahead; we could put most of our men in the trees along the road and leave a small force or some of the wains and horse carts out in the open area to bait them to attack."

"That's a good idea, Henry. I'd been thinking along those lines myself."

Actually, I hadn't been thinking about it at all; I'd already decided to do it. But Henry was right; it was the logical thing to do and something we'd learnt our men and they'd practiced over and over again. Using some of the wains and horse carts to bait Devon's men would be best. The drivers could pretend to run away into the woods and abandon them as Devon's men approached. That would certainly draw Devon's men deeper into our trap; the rest of the galley companies' wains and horse carts could be sent further up the road. It was something we practiced in our "make believe" wars.

****** *Peter*

Henry and I didn't know how much time we had until Devon's forces reached us so we rode as if they were right on our heels. We moved past the column of foot archers at a fast amble, shouting encouragements to them as we did, and continued on until we got to the first open area after the road entered the thick woods.

One look and we knew it wouldn't work. The trees weren't thick enough; there wouldn't be enough cover for our men to hide behind before Devon's men reached the clearing. Our men were sure to be seen and the alarm given before we could spring our trap and destroy them. So I sent my apprentice sergeant back to the column with orders for the companies to keep coming.

The next open area we reached was where the road passed through a little meadow in the forest about a mile further north. It was much better because the forest was thicker and the trees came right up to the edge of the road. The archers could be assigned fighting positions next to the road and then walked back into the thick woods to wait out of sight until their captains and lieutenants called them forward to begin pushing arrows into Devon's men.

Waiting in such positions meant they wouldn't be seen if one of Devon's men happened to go into the trees to shite or run for home.

"This one will work," I shouted as I pulled my horse up in the middle of the little meadow and pointed. "We'll put some carts and wains over there with food and other loot to draw them in and string out the archers on either side of the road all the back to the first clearing."

I immediately pulled my horse's head around and began rapidly moving back to the first of the companies of foot archers coming back north on the road. I was already thinking behind my eyes about where to place the men and wains.

"We'll need to hide one of the companies in the trees on the other side of the meadow in case Devon's men try to break out in that direction," I announced loudly over the sound of our horses' pounding hooves to Henry. He was riding on my right and appeared to be getting tired. So was I. We were starting to get long in the tooth for this sort of thing.

"The company closest to us now that they've reversed direction is Charlie Wright's, isn't it?"

"Aye," Henry agreed as he held his reins with one hand and somehow smoothed his beard with his other hand as he usually does when he wants to ponder something important. "Charlie's company got away last this morning and was at the tail end of the column when the captain turned the foot archers around; so his company should be leading the column now that they are coming back this way."

"Well then," I said, "we better get to Charlie and tell him to march his company all the way through the meadow and set them up in the trees on the other side as a blocking force. We'll stop all the other companies before they reach the meadow and send them into the trees—except for their wains and horse carts; we'll tell them to keep coming."

****** *Henry*

"Assign your men in pairs to positions all along both sides of the road from whence they can get a clear push at anyone on the road in front of them. You're to command the pairs on one side of the road, your lieutenant those you position on the other side. You know what to do after you show each pair of men their position, take them far enough back away from the road so they can't be seen and have them rest and get ready to fight in pairs.

"But remember this—you and your lieutenant are to be the only ones in your company watching the road and you're to be damn careful not to be seen while you do it. If you are seen, fade back into the trees; send your runners back to get your men when you are ready for them to run forward and begin pushing out arrows, not before."

Over and over again Peter and I repeated the order to each company captain and his lieutenant as we assigned their company to the particular stretch of road that would be its ambush position. And over and over again we emphasized that they should wait and not let their men show themselves as Devon's army got deeper and deeper into our trap. And, of course, each was told what to do when Devon's army finally realized they had been caught in an ambush and started to retreat or escape into the woods.

"Rush your men forward and kill as many of Devon's men as you can; and particularly the knights and the mounted men at arms. Let the villagers in the levies scatter and go home unhurt if they throw down their weapons and run, but go for the knights and fighting men even if they run—and try to kill them all. Don't let a one of them escape even if you have to chase them through the woods."

There's no sense in letting them regroup to fight again another day, eh?

Every one of our captains and lieutenants claimed to understand what was expected of him and their men. And so they should—many of them had participated in similar real ambushes over the years and they had all practiced both setting them and escaping from them in the make-believe wars and battles that constantly occur to keep our men busy and trained up when they are not on board their galleys and transports.

What was particularly helpful was that Commander William himself rode in with information about the size of Devon's army and when it might arrive just as Peter and I were getting our last two galley companies into their positions. His news was very encouraging: Devon and his army should reach the woods in about an hour and, at the slow speed they were moving, should reach the meadow where some of our wains and horse carts would appear to be abandoned in a little less than two.

We all immediately turned around and went back up the road together to call the captains and lieutenants out of the trees and tell them what to expect.

"The key thing," William repeated over and over again to each of them before we moved down the road to the next company, "is to let as many of the enemy's men as possible march past you so they get deeper and deeper into our ambush. That means you must not bring your men forward to their positions along the road until the enemy has finished marching past and the road is empty; and, whatever you do, make sure your men don't start pushing arrows at Devon's men until they actually start fleeing back down the road to escape."

Our captains and their lieutenants had been told the same thing many times before in our "make believe" war games; but this was real and they needed to hear it again.

****** *William*

Raymond and his little band of horse archers found the rest of Richard's outriders watching the road from the hillside where Richard said they would find them. He'd gathered them up and ridden down the road a little farther until he'd seen Devon's marching army and how slow it was moving. As a result, Raymond was able to return to my temporary camp with the outriders in plenty of time for me to leave him in command and get myself off to our main force of foot archers. George and Richard had come in about the same time with a complete count of the forces we would be facing. Things looked good.

After talking things over with Raymond, I decided to leave Raymond in command of the horse archers and take personal command of our ambush force—after making sure Raymond and his major knew what they were to do—block the road and kill anyone who tried to resist including Devon and all his knights and mounted men at arms; the villagers in Devon's levies who had dropped their weapons were to be allowed to go home unharmed.

Of course we let them go unharmed; if we were successful they'd soon be tenanting our lands and free, if they so desired, to make their marks on the company's roll and go for an archer or sailor.

George came with me and we rode together to re-join the foot archers at the site of our hoped-for ambush where the road passed through a particularly thick wood. It was a strange ride in that the first hour or so of it was spent riding parallel to the road in order to get ahead of the men at the front of Devon's column. We could periodically see them way off in the distance to our left.

Peter and Henry were dismounted and just finishing the placement of the last of the galley companies in their ambush positions when George and I and our apprentice sergeants reached them. Peter and Henry waved friendly welcomes and their smiles got even bigger when they got the news about the size and the disorganization of Devon's army. So did the smiles of their apprentice sergeants and the company captain and his lieutenant who had been standing in the road listening to them.

"They're about an hour behind us, maybe more," I shouted somewhat gleefully as we rode up. "And moving as slow and stupid as a piece of apple pie; they don't even have any outriders out in front."

Peter and Henry immediately mounted up and we turned around and rode back up the road together to call the captains and lieutenants out of the trees and give them the encouraging news. As we rode from company to company, Peter and Henry told me what they had already ordered and it sounded right proper, and I told them as much. My message to the company captains and lieutenants was a familiar one.

"The main thing," I briefly emphasized to each of the captains and lieutenants as we came to them, "is to let as many of the enemy's men as possible march past you so they get deeper and deeper into our ambush. That means you must hide yourselves so they don't see you and not bring your men back to their fighting positions along the road until Devon's men have finished going past and the road is empty.

"Whatever you do, make sure your men don't start pushing their arrows at Devon's men until they actually start fleeing back down the road to escape—and when they do start running, your men are concentrate on killing the knights and mounted men at arms and ignore the villagers who drop their weapons."

Our captains and their lieutenants had just been told the same thing by Peter and Henry and many times previously in our "make believe" war games; but this was real and they needed to hear it once again. Of course they did.

****** *George*

My father was quite pleased when he saw some of our wains and horse carts at the far end of the meadow. He'd heard the explanation as to why they were there, and been told that the rest of our wains and horse carts had been sent further on up the road beyond the company positioned on the other side of the meadow to stop any escapees trying to break out in that direction.

"An excellent idea, by God, an excellent idea. There's nothing like the possibility of looting someone else's property to attract the men of the village levies, is there?

Seeing the wains with their panic-stricken drivers running away will draw the men at the front of Devon's column into the meadow like cheese draws mice, and those behind them will follow just as sure as God made green apples.

"And you're right that we'll need a steady man here to make sure their drivers all pretend to panic and run away most believable-like. But not you Henry, you're too valuable. I need you in command of the fighting down where the road enters the wood just as Peter will be in command of the fighting at this end of the ambush.

"But I've got just the man for the job—you, Major." He said it with a smile as he pointed at me.

***** *George*

Thomas Young and I got to work as soon my father galloped off with his lieutenants. They were going back to where the road entered the woods to make sure that someone was assigned to gallop up the road shouting warnings to the hidden company captains and lieutenants when the enemy was about to come in sight.

The first thing we did was make sure that there were no weapons left in wagons and horse carts being left in the meadow, but plenty of food and tents and rain skins to attract looters. I also had their drivers reposition some of them towards the back of the meadow where the road re-entered the thick woods. That way more of them would be in the meadow when we sprang the trap.

Then I had another idea—I took the coins in my pouch and spread them between my pouch and Thomas Young's pouch and the pouches of two of the drivers—and hid a pouch in each of the first four wains Devon's column would reach. Finding them, I told a grinning Thomas and their drivers, really ought to set off a rush forward to search the other wains and carts.

And the coins will attract our own men as well; I'll have to watch for that and warn Thomas Young.

Once the carts and wains were placed, and their cargos adjusted to be reasonable bait, I gathered their drivers as a group, divided them into pairs, and explained how they were to act when the first of Devon's men reached the meadow, and then took each of them to a place in the trees where he was to hide his longbow and arrows.

There was a bit of confusion with Charlie Wright, the captain of the company whose men were assigned to hold the area beyond the meadow, but I soon straightened it out. Each of the "fleeing" drivers, including me and Thomas Young, was assigned to run to a pair of Charlie's waiting archers who would have his longbow and arrows waiting for him. Their horses would be left in the traces as prizes to lure Devon's men forward.

It would be up to me, according to my father, to decide when Devon's column was to be attacked and give the order for the attack to begin—when they began to push past the spoils-laden wains and carts and on to the road beyond the meadow.

Chapter Four

The wait is over

My father himself brought the word that the enemy was coming. He and his apprentice sergeant came riding up the road ahoying the captains and lieutenants who were acting as their company's watchers, and shouting that the enemy was on the road and that the front of the enemy column was about to enter the woods.

Each watcher had a couple of men standing by as runners ready to hurry back deeper into the trees to keep his company's waiting archers and sergeants informed—one to tell them to get ready when the final warning came; the second when it was time for the archers to actually come forward to their assigned positions and join the fight.

Conducting an ambush, and escaping from one, was part of what the archers and their sergeants were learnt and had practiced many times. But this was very different—this was real. The only question was how fast something unexpected would occur and what it would be.

My father and his apprentice reached the meadow on their fast-ambling horses, and shouted the news that Devon's army would reach us in about thirty minutes.

"Take care of yourself and your men, George," he said to me with a serious look on his face as he pulled up for a second before he went on up the road to where the rest of our wains and carts were parked. "You're not supposed to stand out here in the open and fight them; so don't wait too long to pretend you are afraid and run to draw them in."

Then he kicked his horse in the ribs and hurried on.

I didn't have time to beg him to be careful himself, and that I already had my men in position and ready to act panic-stricken and run away into the trees; he could see that for himself.

****** *George*

The arrival of Devon's army in the meadow was a surprise even though we knew they were coming. One moment the road was empty and we were anxiously waiting alone by our carts and wains, the next moment there were men on horseback and foot entering the meadow. They were as surprised to see us as we were to see them.

We just stared at each other for a few second. It didn't take long for a couple of them to realize that we were unarmed and begin advancing towards us. Then, like a weir breaking, first one of them and then all of them surged forward.

"Run," I shouted a few seconds later as Thomas Young and I jumped down from the bed of the wain where we'd been waiting and fled into the trees. All around me my archers were making cries of surprise and warning calls—and then bolting for the trees to get away. Several of the drivers started to pull their horses around and try to escape, and then thought better of it and jumped down to flee.

One of the carts overturned as the frightened horse pulling it bolted; and a brace of driverless horses somehow got tangled in the harnesses of another pair. Everywhere there was confusion and running men.

There were no flies on the men who surprised us. As I bolted for the woods, unarmed and waving my arms about in distress, I looked over my shoulder and watched as the Earl of Devon's men ran and galloped into the meadow to see who we might be. Our panicked flight obviously encouraged them.

Within a few brief seconds we were in the woods running for our waiting weapons and they were beginning to reach our wains and carts and climb aboard them to loot their cargos. As you might imagine, the unattended horses in the wain and cart traces became increasingly excited at all the activity and began to bolt.

More and more of the men from Devon's column hurried into the meadow both on foot and, a few, on horseback. There were women and children as well. They all seemed to be hurrying forward to see for themselves what the people walking and riding in front of them had found.

The enthusiasm of Devon's men increased as the first pouch of coins was discovered. The result was much shouting and screaming with every wain and horse cart being quickly chased down and filled with men and women frantically rummaging through its cargo—and triumphantly shouting whenever they found something of value.

In less than two minutes the meadow was packed with people and there was absolute chaos in and around the recently abandoned carts and wains. And it got worse when the horses panicked and some of the wains turned over when their horses got spooked and tried to run away. And it worsened even more when a band of riders, almost certainly the Earl of Devon and some of his knights, forced their way through the rapidly growing mob and tried to restore order and, of course, seize whatever might be of value for themselves.

By the time the Earl and his horsemen reached the abandoned transports, some of the cart and wain horses were being unhitched to be taken as spoils of war, and food and clothing was frantically being thrown out of their cargo beds as more and more people climbed into them and desperately rummaged through them for something to take—and screamed with joy when they made a valuable find, and then fought to keep it from the grasping hands trying to take it away from them.

There were everywhere fights and arguments over the horses and other spoils. The meadow was full of people all trying to get to our transports and those lucky sods who had already gotten their hands on some of whatever our transports were carrying.

The confusion and arguing over the spoils ended, and the real fighting started, because of what one of the looters found in the carts and wains. It was a woman, of all things, who started our attack. She had found the last pouch of coins and jumped down from the horse cart and ran into the trees beyond the meadow in an effort to escape from a couple of men who had seen her find it and were chasing after her to take it—and ran straight into two of Charlie Wright's waiting archers, and then saw many more waiting with their weapons ready.

I was nearby picking up my weapons and saw the whole thing. She was dismayed, the unknown woman was, and just stood there clutching the pouch she had found and staring at the waiting archers with her mouth agape in surprise. The men behind her, however, immediately recognized the danger for what it was. They turned around and began running and shouting to raise the alarm.

They almost made it out of the trees before they went down screaming, one after another, with arrows in their backs. One of them fell to his knees staring in disbelief at the point of the arrowhead on the bloody shaft he was holding with both hands. It had gone all the way through him and was protruding from his chest.

Charlie Wright's archers were ready and waiting. They ran forward at Charlie's shout and immediately began to pour arrows into the disorganized crowd of people in the crowded meadow. There wasn't a one of Charlie's archers who couldn't hit a target anywhere in it. And there were plenty of targets.

I stepped somewhat into the open from behind the tree where I'd been hiding and pushed an arrow into the side of a nearby mounted man with a great black beard on a frightened and rearing horse, apparently a knight from the quality of his tunic and the size of his horse. He was less than twenty paces away from me and spurring his horse in an effort to break through the mob of people in front of him and reach the safety of the road. It was an easy push.

Blackbeard lurched to the side in his saddle as my arrow hit him and dropped his reins immediately. For a few seconds he desperately fumbled at the shaft with one hand and tried to hold on to his saddle with the other, but then a great gush of blood came out of his mouth and he slid off the horse sideways and was trampled by the mob before I could push another heavy into him. His horse crashed over on its side a moment later and I saw people go down under it. I was using heavies with armour piercing points, as were all our men because we had been particularly ordered to go after Devon's knights, but I don't think he was wearing armour.

Everywhere the shrieks of joy and the fights over the spoils changed in seconds to screams of terror and desperate efforts to escape. Some of Devon's people ran into the woods to escape, but most of the people in the square instinctively headed back towards the road they'd just travelled and the safety they imagined was there. Many went down with arrows in their backs and others were trampled.

Within a few seconds there was no one left on horseback and less than a minute later only Devon's dead and wounded were in the meadow. At that point, Charlie Wright's cautiously advancing archers came out of the trees surrounding the meadow and began to pick their way through the carnage.

It was obvious from the sounds that came from farther down the road that a similar fate was befalling the main body of Devon's army, those marching in his column who hadn't yet reached the little meadow to join in the frantic search for spoils. The noise of the fighting went on for a while, and then began to fade away.

****** *William*

We heard the fighting begin about thirty minutes after my apprentice sergeant and I reached the wains and carts that had been driven further on up the road beyond the meadow where my son was waiting for Devon's men. They were the transports carrying each company's additional bales of arrows and the other supplies and equipment that were too important to be left in the meadow as bait. I had already started leading my horse back towards the meadow when I heard the noise and knew the fighting had begun.

John and I immediately dismounted close to the trees by the side of the road, nocked an arrow into our longbows, and waited to see if any of Devon's men were able to breakout through our lines and come this way. Nothing.

After a while we resumed leading our horses down the road towards the meadow—and, because we had no idea as to the outcome of the fighting ahead of us and what we might find, we remained on high alert and ready to either step into the trees and fade out of sight or quickly remount our horses and gallop for safety.

My fears were understandable and groundless. We walked down the road until we could see into the meadow where we'd left the carts and wains to bait Devon's men and I'd last seen George. When we did, we immediately knew that at least this part of the battle had been successful—

because the only men we saw on their feet were a dozen or so archers wearing our distinctive hooded tunics with the stripes of their ranks. They were walking among the bodies of the dead and wounded men littering the meadow and jumped to attention when they saw me.

The three-stripe sergeant in charge of the archers told us that he and his men had been ordered to stay in the meadow to guard the wounded prisoners and had been passing the time by stripping Devon's dead and wounded of their weapons and valuables.

Peter and all the rest of the men in Charlie Wright's company, the sergeant told us, including George and his young apprentice sergeant, had recently begun walking down the road to provide assistance and reinforcements to any of our other companies which might need it. We mounted our horses and rapidly ambled down the road to catch up to them.

It was an interesting ride and what we saw was quite heartening. All along the road between the two meadows we came upon large numbers of Devon's dead, wounded, and captured men being guarded by archers. There were also periodic piles of weapons that had been collected, some horse-drawn carts and wains filled with tents and supplies, and about thirty suits of armour of various qualities.

Included in the spoils we saw in the meadow were about a dozen good horses of the kind favoured by nobles and knights. In addition to those horses, we saw a number of similar horses which appear to have been killed in the brief battle or had been wounded and then mercied to stop their screams.

Finding so many horses was not surprising as our archers had been told to particularly push their arrows at the knights and their horses. What was initially somewhat surprising, until I thought about it, was that there were so few unwounded men among those who had been captured; that, of course, was because the men who were obviously from the village levies had been allowed to throw down their weapons and escape into the woods so they could run to their homes.

What we didn't see were any captured or wounded men who were dressed as if they might be knights; they were all either among the dead men on the road or had escaped into the trees. Devon's wounded men didn't know it yet, but after we finished barbering them we intended to use some of our wains to carry them to their villages and Exeter. Most importantly, the Earl of Devon had not yet been found despite a silver coin being offered to the man who found his body.

Peter and Henry were waiting in the meadow with a large number of our men. And so, to my great relief, was my son. As I rode up, even before a word was spoken, I instinctively knew from everyone's smiles, and from what I'd already seen on the road, that the news was all good—Devon's army had been utterly destroyed.

I immediately sent my apprentice riding off to find Raymond and bring him in for a meeting if he was not actively engaged in fighting or pursuing Devon's survivors. If he was still engaged, John was to join him and assist in any way he could.

******

Raymond and a number of his horse archers rode in about half an hour later and joined us as we inspected our captured weapons and armour. Spirits were high and our earlier decisions were quickly confirmed. Raymond and all of his horse archers and outriders would immediately ride as fast as possible for Exeter to either take possession of Rougemont Castle or put it under siege. They were to leave immediately in an effort to reach Rougemont before word of today's fighting reached its remaining defenders—in the hope that the castle's guard would be down and the drawbridge lowered so our men could ride in and take the castle before its defenders knew what was happening.

Two galley companies of foot archers, the first two on the road, would also leave immediately and also begin marching to Exeter at their highest possible speed. When they arrived, they would either replace the horse archers holding Rougemont or join them in putting it under siege.

George was to go with Raymond to command the siege if one was needed. I, on the other hand, would begin marching the bulk of our army and the outriders towards Windsor. Hopefully, we would get there before King John had to come out to meet with the barons. Henry and Peter would march with me. Richard would accompany George as his second. Most of the outriders, however, would come with us in the main column under Richard's lieutenant.

Once Rougemont was either taken or successfully under siege, Raymond and most of his horse archers, all of the horse archers he didn't think were needed in Exeter for the siege, would ride to catch up with our main force. If there was a siege, George and Richard would stay to command the siege which would be laid on the castle by the two foot companies and whatever number of horse archers Raymond decided should remain with them; if there was no siege, George and Richard would stay at Rougemont only long enough to make sure the castle could withstand one and then hurry to rejoin us.

We'd already spent some time speculating out loud as to how long a siege might last if we had to start one. And, of course we had no answers; it would depend on how much food was in the castle and how many defenders and servants were inside to help eat it.

One of our spies in Exeter, the old archer and his wife operating the alehouse in Exeter, had told us in the past that Rougemont Castle didn't have much in the way of siege supplies in its storerooms. But that, we knew all too well, might have changed when Devon decided to leave the safety of his castle and march his army off to war. We keep enough food in each of our castles to withstand a siege for at least a year, but that's because our relief force might have to come all the way from Cyprus and take months to gather.

Raymond's plan was to ride all night and send a very small advance force of volunteers over the Rougemont drawbridge when it was lowered in the morning and the gate was opened to admit the castle's servants. Sending a large number of men wouldn't work because their approach might alert the guards and cause the drawbridge to be raised. The advance force would try to seize and hold the gate until reinforcements arrived, much as we had done a few years ago in Tunis and Algiers.

"I don't want you and George to be among the men who try to take the castle's entrance by surprise," I told Raymond. "It'll be dangerous and you're both too valuable." *I remember poor Randolph, don't I?*

And I did even more; after the meeting, while the horse archers were getting ready to mount up and leave, I took Raymond aside and told him that if it became necessary to lay a siege on Rougemont, I wanted him to leave at least ten extra horse archers under a very dependable sergeant. They could ride to Windsor with George after it was taken.

Of course, I did; I wasn't about to have George riding alone to Windsor after Rougemont was captured. England's roads were nowhere safe for a solitary traveller, even an experienced fighting man with a remount.

Raymond nodded his understanding most soberly, and agreed without saying a word. It was with a heavy heart and a strange sense of foreboding that I watched my son ride off with the horse archers a few minutes later. I knew Raymond. He was not the sort of man who would send his men into battle and watch from afar. Neither was George.

Chapter Five

Rougemont Castle

I divided the archers into three armies as soon as the battle was over. Two of them immediately began to the march towards Windsor to fulfil our contract by protecting the king. Henry and I led the largest army, nine galley companies of foot archers and most of Richard's outriders under his lieutenant.

We began marching north towards Okehampton. From there we'd turn east and march towards Windsor on the London road. Richard and several of his veteran outriders were not with us; Raymond needed them, at least temporarily, for their knowledge of where Rougemont is in relation to Exeter and the London road. Richard and his outriders, it seems, had ridden some of their watching patrols all the way to within sight of the castle.

Our second army of seven galley companies of foot archers under Peter's command also began marching north. It was immediately ahead of us and was pulling further and further ahead as they were making a forced march and moving as fast as possible. They will be on the road ahead of us until they reach where the cart path from Cornwall joins the main road to London near Okehampton.

At the intersection is where our armies would separate. Henry and I would march our army east towards Windsor and London; Peter and his men, on the other hand, would turn west and make a forced march towards Cornwall on the cart road in order to return to Restormel and their galleys moored along the river. They can rest their legs after they arrive at Restorml, for as soon as they arrive they will immediately board their galleys and sail and row for London.

Henry and I were marching behind them and going slower in order to pace our men who have much further to walk.

If the winds are favourable, Peter and his men should reach London and the king and Thomas at Windsor before the main body of our troops who are marching overland to Windsor on the London road. A messenger has been sent ahead to Restormel to announce their coming so that Harold could have the galleys on the Fowey fully provisioned and ready to cast off the moment they arrive.

The seriously wounded prisoners will stay at Okehampton for barbering or burying as the case may be. Our own casualties were very light; a few wounded men. We've already loaded those who can't continue into a wain and sent it north to Okehampton with a strong escort.

Raymond and George and Raymond's horse archers, on the other hand, were not marching with either of our two main armies. They were part of a smaller third army commanded by Raymond and already on the road riding south to Rougemont with two companies of foot archers following along as fast as possible behind them. They'd arrive sometime tomorrow, hopefully before word reaches Exeter that Devon's army has been defeated.

Whether or not Raymond and George would be able turn around and catch up with me and Henry whilst we are still marching on Windsor depends on whether or not they are able to take Rougemont by surprise. If not, some of them will have to remain to lay on a siege. If the castle is taken quickly, on the other hand, one of the two companies of foot archers and some of the horse archers will be left to garrison it, and Raymond and George and the rest of their men will ride hard for Windsor and, hopefully, arrive to reinforce us before King John meets the barons.

If Rougemont is not immediately taken, George will stay to command the siege, with Richard as his second. Raymond, on the other hand, will stay only so long as he thinks he and his horse archers are needed in Exeter; then he will ride for Windsor with most of his horse archers leaving only a few of his men with George and Richard to act as the castle's outriders.

Raymond knows I want his horse archers with us when we arrive at Windsor in order to discourage the barons from attacking by presenting the greatest possible show of force. As a result, I don't expect him to stay in Exeter for more than a day or two—just long enough to identify and wipe out any potential relief force that might be formed to break the siege if we have to impose one.

Of course, dividing one's fighting force is usually not a good idea, but I felt I had no choice; we want to honour our contract with the king, but we want Rougemont even more. Fortunately, there is not likely to be much opposition to our taking Rougemont since we so soundly destroyed Devon's army and his allies will undoubtedly want to use their men to defeat King John rather than use them to rescue Rougemont for Devon's heirs. If we discourage the barons from attacking John and they decide to use some of their army to retake Rougemont, we'll do whatever it takes to prevent its recapture by the barons—or the king, even if it means fighting them all.

****** *George*

Uncle Raymond had a plan to take Rougemont, and he told Richard and me all about it as we and his entire company of horse archers rode rapidly south towards Exeter with some of our wains and carts clattering along with us. Coming along behind us are two companies of foot archers engaged in a forced march with periodic double-timing in an effort to arrive and reinforce the horse archers as soon as possible. They've got a couple of horse carts and wains with them to pick up anyone who falls out for some reason.

It was interesting to ride with the horse archers by the light of the moon. There were light-hearted and not so light-hearted complaints about sore arses and twice rumours swept through the column about a horse going down and breaking a leg, but no one complained about the discomfort and dangers of a forced march in the dark; even the newest recruits understood the need to get to Rougemont before its defenders got word of Devon's defeat and began taking steps in an effort to fight us off—such as laying in siege supplies, raising the castle's drawbridge, closing the gate, and manning the battlements.

Uncle Raymond obviously understood this. Accordingly, he told us, he intends to make an effort to take the castle by surprise as soon as we arrive. His plan is for an innocent-appearing horse-drawn cart with a single volunteer driver, and ten heavily armed archers lying on top of one another as its cargo, to drive up to gate as if they were delivering supplies—and jump out and take it and hold it open until reinforcements arrive.

Another wain with more archers will be a minute behind the first, just far enough back so that they didn't appear to be arriving together and arouse suspicions. And then a third wain will come in right behind the second.

"The horse cart with the first ten men hidden in it will start forward as soon as we see that the castle gate is open and the drawbridge down, as it would normally be during the day so that people can go back and forth and food and firewood delivered," he explained.

"The next two transports carrying the first reinforcements will follow close behind, but not too close so as to arouse the castle and cause the drawbridge to be raised.

"Thirty men should be more than enough to hold the gate open and keep the drawbridge down until the rest of the horse archers can gallop into the bailey and join the fight," he told us.

It was, of all things, Uncle Raymond told us, a plan based on an old story about a siege in Greece that Uncle Thomas had read in one of the monastery's books before he came to get my father and they went for archers. We'd all heard it him tell it many times. It succeeded then; hopefully it would succeed again.

As soon as Uncle Raymond explained his plan, Richard and I understood why he had insisted on bringing so many empty wains and horse carts as well as extra horses to pull them and extra wheels to repair them—the wheels of wains and horse carts and the horses pulling them are constantly breaking down and he wanted to make sure at least three of the transports would be able to make it to Exeter and capable of going straight to the castle.

Besides, if our surprise attack on Rougemont fails and the city of Exeter closes its gates to us so we can't buy from its merchants, we'll need them to carry food and supplies when we go foraging.

Sure enough, a few minutes later I heard a loud, sharp noise as a wain travelling behind me hit a hole in the road and one its front wheels broke apart. I followed Uncle Raymond as he rode back to see what happened—all the time shouting "Keep moving, step it up, faster lads, keep moving." The sergeants repeated the order and the column increased its speed.

Less than a minute later, my apprentice sergeant and I listened as a file of horse archers under a sergeant named "Jimmy" were ordered to pull the wain off to the side of the road, replace the wheel, and re-join the column as soon as possible. It was the second broken wheel of the night and, according to Richard, we are still some hours away from reaching Rougemont Castle.

Part of the problem, of course, is that the men driving the wain and cart horses cannot see the holes in the road in time to avoid them, especially when a cloud is passing in front of the moon.

****** *George*

We rode all night without stopping. In the morning we began to encounter people walking on the road and see others walking on the footpaths and working in the fields on either side of the road. We also met a few carts and wains coming towards us which quickly pulled off the road to let us pass.

The traffic on the road was all very normal and most of the people who saw us were serfs and slaves going about their normal daily chores. But they inevitably stopped and looked at us with great interest. Several hundred fast-moving riders accompanied by horse carts and wains was not a common sight on this road or any other.

Orders had been passed down the column several times about what to do and say when the sun came up and we began encountering people on the road—"smile and be friendly. And if anyone inquires, say we are going to Exeter to take boats to the war in France and ask for their good wishes and prayers."

Chapter Six

We have a go at Rougemont.

The mid-day sun was just beginning to pass overhead when, in the distance off to our left, we began to see Rougemont Castle emerging through the trees. The castle was quite large and imposing. It quickly became clear to me and everyone around me that Rougemont was a strong fortress and would never be taken by a direct assault; we'd either gull our way in or we'd have to besiege the castle and wait until its defenders were starved out.

The night's hard and boring ride was behind me and my hunger from not breaking my morning fast was forgotten; I was wide awake and ready to go. And, from the looks of them, so too were the men with whom I had been riding. But there was a problem, a big problem—we had ridden too far forward towards the castle.

Uncle Raymond immediately moved the column back until the castle could no longer be seen. His reasoning was sound and quickly understood and appreciated by the men who hurried to obey—if we could see Rougemont in the distance well enough through the trees to be impressed by its size and strength, someone on its walls might be able see us on the road and sound the alarm.

From now until the signal was given for the horse archers to charge forward without their supply horses, only the three transports, two small horse carts and a wain, carrying the thirty men of our assault force would move closer until the gate is taken; the rest of the horse archers would come at a gallop as soon as the assault force had taken the gate by surprise.

"Uncle Raymond," I said as everyone stiffly dismounted and began pissing after many hours of riding, "I need to be the driver or one of the archers in the first cart so the men will respect me." I said it as I shook my dingle and watched as his apprentice sergeant handed him an old linen corn sack that turned out to be full of ragged clothes.

Uncle Raymond looked at me, shook his head, and muttered one word—"No."

I wasn't the only one to ask; I'd heard Richard and several of the sergeants make the same request hours ago. They had been similarly denied.

***** *George*

My request to lead the assault on Rougemont was summarily refused without an explanation. Uncle Raymond didn't say why, but I could see my father's hand in his decision.

I could hardly complain, however, not when Uncle Raymond announced that he himself would be driving the first ten men to the castle gate and would be doing so in the smallest two-wheeled horse cart that was available. I was content, however—I am to drive the second transport, one of the wains, and Richard the third, another small cart.

"That way," Uncle Raymond explained with a smile. "I can tell your father that you and I were only the drivers, not part of the attack force."

We three drivers are each going to drive up to the castle wearing clothes appropriate for village cart and wain drivers—the rags Uncle Raymond had his apprentice sergeant strip off some the dead men from Devon's levies.

The ten archers who would ride in each of the transports had long ago been named. They, of course, would not have to change clothes; they and their tunics and weapons would be hidden under the ragged linen or leather covers that every cart and wain uses to protect its cargo from rain.

Uncle Raymond had obviously been thinking about taking Rougemont Castle whilst the rest of us were congratulating each other about our victory. And he was right; it certainly wouldn't do for someone to drive a wain or horse cart up to the Rougemont drawbridge wearing an archer's tunic and carrying weapons.

Richard and I quickly followed Uncle Raymond's lead and immediately took off our tunics and began rummaging through the rags to find some clothes that would cover my chain shirt and wrist knives. They were all as filthy and smelled as terrible as you might expect from men who worked in the fields and never took off their clothes. My clothes were hardly ever so foul, all thanks to Beth and Becky who every so often finished sewing a new tunic for me and gave away my old ones after boiling them to kill the smell and the lice that had inevitably accumulated to foul them.

Richard and Uncle Thomas had seen me with my wrist knives many times, but many of the men standing around me had not. The horse archers were absolutely fascinated and nudged each other to look when I took off my tunic and pants to put on some of the captured rags; I was similarly surprised when Richard took off his tunic to put on his rags and I saw that he too was wearing a chain shirt and had a pair of concealed knives strapped to his wrists.

Whilst the three of us were dressing in the filthy rags appropriate for the wain and cart drivers of Devon, the carefully selected men in the three assault parties were climbing into the three horse-drawn transports with their weapons and making ribald jokes about being jammed together on top of one another. Once they were in place, willing hands pulled a tent over them to hide them as would normally be the case with a cargo its driver was trying to protect it from the rain.

Uncle Raymond's cart was particularly full. The archers were stretched out two and three deep on top of each other and the length of the cart's bed was so short that their tent-covered sandaled feet hung out over the end.

If I hadn't seen it for myself, I never would have believed that so many heavily armed men could ever be carried in a small horse cart with a ragged-appearing eleventh man driving the horse. I could only hope that the little cart full of heavily armed archers surprised the guards at the castle's gate as much as it surprised me that so many men could fit into the back of such a small cart.

One thing is sure, however; it's unlikely a horse cart has ever before carried such a lethal cargo—every man of them had climbed in with both a longbow and either a short sword or a bladed pike.

More importantly, one look at the men as they climbed into the wains and laid themselves down on top of one another, I instinctively knew that Raymond had selected them because they truly knew how to use their weapons. The long wooden handles of their pikes hung far out over the back of the cart and looked quite innocent; building materials perhaps.

It was as the men were settling themselves and being covered that we suddenly realized that we had a new problem—the handful of men and women walking on the road and on the footpaths leading to the castle could see that we had moved back and were getting ready for a fight. Many of them were obviously villagers who worked as servants in the castle or serfs and slaves coming and going from their fields. They could sound the alarm, and likely would if something wasn't done quickly. Uncle Raymond recognized the problem.

"Stop them if you can," Uncle Raymond shouted over his shoulder as he flicked his whip on the horse's arse and his cart lurched forward. The sun had been up for hours; the castle's drawbridge should be down and its gate open— unless we'd been seen from the castle walls or one of the walkers we'd encountered had somehow gotten past us and sounded the alarm.

****** *George*

I ran to my nearby wain when Uncle Raymond's cart started forward. It was only a few steps away and I quickly swung myself on to the rough board where the driver sits in front of the wain's cargo bed.

It was early in the afternoon and visibility was good despite the clouds overhead. The excited archers in the wain were already pulling the tent over themselves as I grabbed the reins from the horse archer who'd been holding them to keep the horse steady while the archers assigned to it climbed aboard. He wished me a cheerful and sincere "good fortune" and jumped down as I flicked the reins to get the wain horse moving.

We lurched forward to follow Uncle Raymond's horse cart and I immediately slumped down, as I'd been told, to make it look like I was half asleep instead of how I felt, which was so excited that I actually began trembling for a few seconds.

Ahead of me I could see Uncle Randolph had his horse trotting so that he was moving briskly as he turned off the Exeter road and on to the cart path leading up to the castle. Richard and I held back as we had been ordered so that we would not appear to be traveling together, and certainly not with innocent-appearing little horse cart traveling ahead of us on the road.

A minute or two later I too turned off the road and on to the cart path that ran up to the castle's gate and the village near it. As soon as I did, I began to encounter men and women walking to and from the castle. I smiled and nodded and lifted a friendly but weary hand to acknowledge their greetings. Ahead of me I could see Uncle Raymond and his horse cart. And I could see the drawbridge over the castle's moat—it was down.

Thank you Jesus and all the saints.

A man carrying a load of firewood on his back had obviously just walked over the drawbridge and was now walking through the castle gate and into the bailey. If the bridge had been up, I would have stopped and waited while Uncle Raymond tried to talk it down in order to "deliver the supply of corn and butter the earl had ordered."

"So far, so good lads," I said as I bent down and spoke under my arm towards the men jammed in behind me in what I hoped was a loud enough whisper for them to hear.

"The drawbridge is down and the gate is open. We've turned off the road and are now on the cart path leading up to the castle. People are walking around us. They look to be castle folk coming and going from their work. None of them looks alarmed and none of them are carrying weapons."

All of a sudden I was jerked away from talking and watching Uncle Raymond approach the castle's drawbridge when I realized that the young man I was passing, a stable boy from the looks of him, intended to jump aboard for a ride to the castle.

"Hey," I shouted at him as I flicked the horse with the driver's whip to get it to trot and then sort of shook it at him. "Don't even think about it. I'm carrying people with the pox for barbering."

I don't know why I said that, about the pox I mean, but it worked. The lad stepped away with a shocked look on his face and stood watching as my horse picked up speed and began trotting even faster. It was, I had decided without even thinking about it, better to catch up with Uncle Raymond and the horse cart than have someone climb aboard and sound the alarm; I don't know what would have actually happened if he had jumped aboard. Nothing good; that's for sure.

But why wasn't he out with Devon?

"Hey?" I turned around and shouted to the lad with my best imitation of a Devon accent. "Why aren't you with the earl and his army?" He didn't answer and I didn't slow down.

Behind me I could see Richard and his wain. His horse was now trotting; he was trying to maintain the distance between us. Uncle Raymond was now only about a thousand paces ahead of us and I was beginning to catch up. There was no one walking nearby so I slowed my horse down to a walk.

"Steady lads, Commander Raymond's cart is just about to reach the drawbridge and the gate into the bailey is still open."

****** *George*

I held my breath as up ahead of me Uncle Raymond began crossing the drawbridge and then passed through gate and entered the bailey. I saw the tent covering the archers in the cart thrown off just as the cart passed through the open gate and entered the bailey.

"They're in the bailey," I shouted with great excitement and enthusiasm as I whipped up the wain horse and kept whipping her until she broke into a lumbering gallop. "Come out and get ready." *God this is exciting.*

I didn't have to tell my passengers twice. The tent covering the archers was instantly thrown off so strongly that it went flying all the way out of the wain. It was quite chaotic behind me and the wain rocked a bit as every man tried to sit up holding his bow in one hand and his drawn sword or bladed pike in the other and they all struggled to get to their knees and be ready to jump out.

As you might imagine every man's eyes including mine were on the fast approaching drawbridge and gate. I darted a quick look behind me and saw that he too had whipped his horse into a gallop and the men in his wain were struggling to sit up and get ready in his cart's little cargo bed.

We clattered from the cart path up on to the thick wooden planks of the drawbridge with such a great bump that for a moment I was afraid we'd break a wheel and turn over. But we didn't. We clattered across the bridge, and bounced hard once again as the wain came off the thick wooden planks of the drawbridge and its wheels dropped back on to the ground, first the two in front and then the back pair.

A few seconds later we passed through the castle's open gate and entered the bailey. As we did we almost ran over two of the archers from Uncle Raymond's horse cart. They were running as fast as they could towards us. It was instantly clear that they had been sent to secure the gate and the crank that must be turned to raise the drawbridge. They were ready to fight with their longbows and an arrow in one hand and their swords clutched in the other.

There was nobody in the bailey except archers, not even a dead body or anyone being held as a prisoner. Everyone must have fled. My men were shouting encouragements to each other and jumping out of the wain long even before I was able to pull up the horse and the wain stopped rolling.

One of them took a nasty fall, but they were all out of wain and on the ground and ready to fight by the time I had the horse stopped and reached behind me to grab my bow and quiver and jumped down to follow them—and saw no one who needed killing and no sign of Uncle Raymond.

The castle's great crenelated battlements were also empty except for a couple of archers who were running along the top of the wall and just disappearing from view as they rounded a corner so that the great stone keep blocked them from view.

What I did see, and it caught my attention, were the backs of a couple of archers, obviously some of the men from Uncle Raymond's horse cart, entering the castle's keep through a narrow door, a door that almost certainly led into the castle's great hall. A few seconds later Richard's wain careened into the bailey and almost ran me over. We didn't pause to exchange greetings.

"Into the keep, lads, take the keep" I shouted as I spun around and began to run towards the open door to enter the keep as Richard and his men leaped out of their horse cart even before it stopped rolling. I could just as well have saved my breath; most of my men were already running for the door and the first of them were already disappearing inside. Out of the corner of my eye I saw and heard the excited horse I'd been driving bolt and the wain turn over with a great crash.

I rushed into the great hall and once again found no enemies to fight. There seemed to be shouting and red faced archers everywhere and no one to oppose them. Some of them were already hurrying down the narrow rounded stairs from the earl's private rooms above the great hall. Uncle Raymond was still not to be seen.

"Where's the lieutenant?" I shouted without addressing anyone in particular. In the excitement of the moment I had forgotten our new ranks.

Then I heard great shouts and the pounding of hooves as the rest of the horse archers galloped in and skittish horses and shouting men began filling the bailey. A few seconds later I heard a great banging sound as the castle gate was closed behind them and the familiar squeaking and squealing sound of a drawbridge being raised.

There was no doubt about it, we had gotten into Rougemont with our deception and taken it without a fight. The castle guards and other possible defenders must have gone off with the earl to march to Windsor in his ill-fated army.

Chapter Seven

The prisoners.

I bounded up the stairs to see for myself what was there—and came face to face with a couple of scared and trembling servant women and a family that was obviously Devon's, three terrified and weeping young girls hiding behind their white-faced mother who had her arms spread wide to hold them safely behind her. An archer with a drawn sword was poking at their beds and another was looking into a couple of chests whose lids were raised.

"Downstairs on the double," I snarled at the two archers. "These people are no threat." I gave the woman a half-hearted nod of acknowledgment and hurried back down the stairs. Someone was shouting my name.

"And you two," I said to the excited two-stripe archer I met half way down the stairs and the one-striper coming up immediately behind him. "You two guard the women and children up there. Stay with them until I relieve you. I'll see you both hanged, if you desert them or let anyone harm them or pillage their belongings."

Both men's eyes widened at my order and the intensity of my venomous threat, but they nodded and the two-striper knuckled his head and repeated it back to me as he should. I didn't say a word when he finished, I nodded in agreement as I just pushed past them on the narrow staircase and continued winding my way down it in the dim light. They looked dependable and probably were since Uncle Raymond had selected them for the assault force.

I don't know why, but for some reason I was greatly concerned behind my eyes about Devon's women and children. Probably because I have young daughters myself and still remember what happened to Lord Edmund's wife and daughters when I was a lad. Strangely enough, I can hardly remember what they looked like, Lord Edmund's family I mean.

****** *George*

As soon as the castle was secured and its battlements manned, Uncle Raymond, Richard, and I began a systematic search of the great castle with several dozen of our hastily gathered men following us. We decided to start in the one place we hadn't yet searched, the castle's dungeons and the food larders we expected to be in them.

We didn't know what we would find, if anything, in the dungeons so we went down the stone steps warily holding candle lanterns in one hand and swords in the other. Would they be as extensive as those of Launceston? Was there an escape tunnel we would need to guard in order to prevent a counter-attack? There were many unknowns that our spies in Exeter had not been able to tell us about.

A big burley two-stripe archer named Edward went down the dungeon stairs first carrying a short sword and galley shield, both of which he clearly knew how to use. I followed immediately behind him carrying a candle lantern. I held it as high as possible so that some of the light would come over Edward's shoulder and he could see what was immediately ahead of him.

As a result, my hand periodically scraped the rough stone ceiling. I hardly noticed. It was a discomfort I had to endure because holding the candle lantern as high as possible was the only way Edward could see. I held my sword in my other hand but dangling down towards the stone stairs to avoid stabbing Edward by mistake.

Raymond and a number of sword carrying archers were immediately behind us with each man holding on to the tunic of the man in front of him with one hand and holding his sword in the other. No one spoke. The further down the stairs we went, the more it got cooler and cooler and the more it smelled damp and foul.

Edward wasn't taking any chances, and rightly so because we had no idea as to what we might encounter; he moved slowly down the extremely narrow and winding stone stairs in the dark, very slowly, one step at a time with his sword ready. It was dark and damp as the light from the candle lamp I was carrying behind him flickered and cast strange shadows. It was deathly quiet.

We reached the bottom of the stairs and entered a narrow tunnel with a low and rounded ceiling. There was the sound of dripping of water somewhere in front of us as well as the rustle of rats scurrying ahead of us. *This place needs some cats, that's for sure.*

Almost immediately we reached what appeared to be some kind of store room for food. I moved the lantern about and we could see what appeared to be empty amphoras along both walls and a couple of empty wooden crates. There was also a small stack of old firewood and some iron hooks sticking out of the wall of the kind hinds and cows might be hung whilst they cured, or perhaps pigs and sheep; I couldn't tell and we didn't stop to look except to see that they were empty.

If this is the castle's larder, it certainly wasn't prepared for tonight's meal, let alone a siege, was the thought behind my eyes as I passed through the little room and ducked my head to enter the tunnel that began again beyond it; our strongholds are required to have at least a year's supply of corn and firewood for two hundred people.[i]

******* *George*

A voice! I distinctly heard a man cough and a muffled voice somewhere ahead of us. And then someone shouted and there was a muffled but clearly angry response and more distant voices. Everyone froze.

Behind me I heard Uncle Raymond say, in a very low whisper, "Steady lads, no one make a sound or move. Pass the lantern back, George; and then you and Edward feel your way forward nice and slow for a look. We'll stay here for a while and be quiet. Fall back if there's trouble."

I slowly handed the lantern back to Uncle Raymond, and Edward and I began inching forward. Actually Edward inched forward into the darkness with his free hand held out in front of him as far as he could reach and his sword hand back so far that it touched me; I held tight to his tunic and shuffled forward when he did.

Of course he held his sword hand back. He didn't want the sword point to make a noise by hitting something he couldn't see. It might alert whoever was in front of us; besides, holding his left hand out and his right with the sword point back meant he could push it straight forward with his full force if someone bumped into us in the dark.

Edward suddenly froze; his hand had touched a wall. I felt it with my sword carrying elbow a moment later. The tunnel had turned hard to the left. Once we got all the way around the corner we could see a dim light ahead of us and the sound of voices became much louder although still not loud enough to be able to understand what was being said.

I suddenly felt such a tremendous need to piss that I almost pulled Edward to stop and lifted my tunic. But I didn't.

We moved slowly and silently in the dark towards the light at the end of the tunnel. As we got closer I could see the flickering shapes of figures moving in a fairly large room ahead of us. Suddenly there was a loud and agonizing scream.

A few second later we could see the room by the light of a candle lantern hanging from a hook on the wall near the entrance to the tunnel—and a naked and sobbing man chained to the left wall with two men in front of him. They were torturing him.

One of the torturers reached forward with something in his hand as Edward reached the entrance to the room and there was another piercing scream. One of the men moved as I slipped into the room behind Edward and let loose of Edward's tunic. Suddenly Edward was not blocking my view, I could see more clearly in the flickering light. I was jolted by what I saw: The torturers were wearing priests' robes—and from the looks on their faces they were enjoying what they were doing.

One of the priests, the shorter of the two, reached out toward the chained and sobbing man who desperately twisted to avoid his outstretched arm.

"That's enough. Stop," I shouted. I couldn't contain myself. Edward spoke at almost the same moment and said almost the same thing, except he added "Or I'll kill you" and said it so slowly and emphatically and with such determination that I knew he truly meant it. There was real hostility in his voice.

Both of the priests whirled around to face us with looks of absolute astonishment on their faces. One of them, the bigger of the two, screamed in surprise at the sound of our voices.

"Who are you?" the little one suddenly demanded as he leaned towards us in an effort to see us better. "We're doing God's work here; so you'll leave and keep your mouth shut if you know what's good for you." Behind me I could hear footsteps. Uncle Raymond must have heard the screams and started forward.

The little priest started towards the tunnel entrance and the nearby candle lantern as he said it. He intended to run for it.

I stepped forward to stand in front of the candle lantern and pointed the tip of my sword at where I thought his belly might be under his robe. He jumped back with a start and raised a placating hand.

"Here, none of that, we're priests aren't we? You can see that, can't you? So put down your sword; it's God's Will that priests not be harmed, isn't it?"

He spoke to me in French. I ignored his questions and responded in English.

"And who is your victim and why are you torturing him? And where is the key to unlock his chains?" I said it sternly as I moved menacingly forward and the little priest moved back to avoid being pricked in his stomach.

"He's the earl's prisoner, that's who he is," the priest said petulantly. "And we're the earl's gaolers and charged with punishing him, so you best not interfere if you know what's good for you."

"There are only two of them," the big priest said to the little priest in Latin. "Let's try to talk them into lowering their swords and walking out of here with us. We can arrest them later."

"Maybe we should run for the tunnel as soon as they sheathe their swords," the little priest responded, also in Latin. "If you can get to the lantern and knock it over, we can run; we know the passage way better than they do."

I responded scornfully in Latin as I watched the chained man as he gasped and tried to pull himself to his feet.

"Don't even think about it," I said. "The tunnel behind us is filled with at least twenty heavily armed men. You two are dead for sure if you don't throw down your knives and torture tools and hand me the key to your prisoner's chains."

"Uncle Raymond," I shouted a moment later. "Please come forward. Everything is under control." *Actually, you two are already dead men; you just don't know it yet.* My call was quite unnecessary. I could tell from the approaching sound of the steps in the tunnel that he would be here momentarily.

"Who are you?" the little priest asked again, this time with much more anxiety and concern in his voice.

****** *George*

So many archers crowded into the torture room that Uncle Raymond had to send most of them back to wait at the entrance. An hour later, it was the two priests who were chained to the wall and the prisoner had been freed. So were two other prisoners.

We found the two other prisoners barely unconscious and left to die in the corner of one of the dungeon's two wet and filthy cells. The archers carried all three of the men into the castle's great hall for food, barbering, and questioning.

One of them died, or perhaps was already dead, but the other two were almost hysterically grateful at their unexpected freedom and a great source of information. Words poured out of them in torrents as they guzzled bowls of morning ale and stuffed bread and cheese into their mouths.

The earl, it seems, had recently brought seven prisoners to Rougemont on a boat. All were English sailors who had been periodically preying on French shipping and the villages along the coast of Normandy from the island of Sark—for King John. Their captain had been a former monk by the name of Eustace.

"Eustace was a fine sailor man and captain and we took many a French prize, but he turned away from us betrayed us," one of the men explained. "The Earl of Devon and some English barons came to Sark on their way to

England from France and convinced him to change sides, to join them and the French and go against the king."

"Aye, that he did," chimed in the other. "Eustace called everyone together and said that anyone who didn't want to fight against the King John could return to England. Seven of us decided to leave and the Earl said we could sail with him to Exeter and make our way home from there. We were in Guernsey at the time, but as soon as we left Guernsey the earl made us prisoners and brought us here to be tortured. The three of us are all that's left."

Chapter Eight

Getting things organized.

There had been no time for courtesies when Uncle Raymond first met the earl's wife, Lady Margaret. He and some of the men from his horse cart had rushed up the stairs from the castle's great hall and into the room where she and her daughters lived because they were in search of the castle's defenders. And, of course, they left immediately to search elsewhere when they didn't find anyone to kill or capture.

Everything was much more relaxed when Uncle Raymond returned later that afternoon with me and Richard in tow immediately after we finished thoroughly inspecting the castle. By then it was increasingly clear to all of us that the Earl of Devon was quite a fool; he had arrogantly assumed that no one would dare try to take his powerful hold, and had gone off with his men and left it virtually undefended.

Even worse for the earl, and better for us, he had left no orders for its elderly constable, apparently a distant relative who was off somewhere tending to his manor, to keep the castle's gate closed and its drawbridge raised while he was away with his army.

****** *George*

Tough and gruff Uncle Raymond was surprisingly gentle with Lady Margaret and her daughters the second time he climbed the stairs to their room. At his request, she stepped out on to the stairs so the children would not hear his news. That's when he informed her that her husband had likely been killed in battle yesterday. All in all, she took it quite well; almost too well, actually. And then we questioned her.

What she told us was not surprising. What we later decided was surprising was that she did not seem particularly distressed when Uncle Raymond told her that her husband had probably been killed and buried where he fell. She told us she knew about the prisoners we found in dungeon, but not who they were or why they were being held. And yes, her husband had called in his knights and village levies and gone off to join a war against King John because of his taxes and scutages.

"And where is the entrance to the castle's escape tunnel, dear lady? We know there is one." *Actually we didn't know that Rougemont had an escape tunnel. Uncle Raymond lied to her because it seemed likely that such a great castle would have one.*

Lady Margaret said she didn't know of an escape tunnel, which was hard for us to believe. Indeed, her claim not to know about an escape tunnel coupled with her lack of distress at hearing that we had probably killed her husband and buried him in an unmarked grave worried us, though we didn't share our worries with her or with each other at the time. Could it mean that she knew the Earl of Devon was still alive and had somehow escaped out from under our noses?

Uncle Raymond told her she would have to leave Rougemont and offered to send her and her daughters to her family in France instead of holding them for ransom. And once again she raised our suspicions by saying that she and her daughters preferred to stay in England.

We left Lady Margaret with a dismayed look on her face and Uncle Raymond's order ringing in her ears; she was to begin packing her personal belongings for transportation to France in the morning.

****** *George*

"Come on, lads. We'll talk to the servants. They know everything," Uncle Raymond said to us as we clattered down the stairs to the great room where they had been assembled. They did indeed know about the castle's escape tunnel and, confirming our suspicions, they told us that Lady Margaret knew all about it as well.

The entrance to escape tunnel, they told us, began at the back of the castle's larder which was in a stone-walled cellar under the keep out by the cook house. We immediately found the poorly concealed tunnel and cautiously walked its long distance carrying candle lanterns until it came out of the ground in an old burial crypt in the midst of a grove of trees some distance from the castle.

We couldn't tell if the escape tunnel had been used recently, but we weren't about to take any chances; some of our archers were immediately set to filling in part of it so it couldn't be used to bring enemy soldiers into Rougemont to suddenly launch a surprise attack on our garrison. Now would-be attackers would have to dig it out in order to gain entrance to the castle, and that would take time and make noise to alert our garrison. And, of course, we would have to dig it out to escape if the castle was ever about to fall to a siege.

After much talking among ourselves that afternoon, another intense inspection of the castle, and a second close questioning the castle's servants, Uncle Raymond decided that it was such a strong castle that only one of the two companies marching to relieve us would be needed to hold the castle even if Devon was still alive and returned with a large army. Accordingly, a small party of horse archers was sent north to tell one of the companies of foot archers to keep coming and the other to turn around on the road and begin the long march to Windsor.

Some of the horse archers, Uncle Raymond announced, would stay with company marching for Windsor to be its outriders and couriers; the rest would return to the castle with the foot archers marching to join us.

"That settles it," Uncle Raymond said to me as we finished inspecting the escape tunnel which the earl's wife denied knowing about, and a party of archers began temporarily filling in. "We're sending Lady Margaret and her children to France tomorrow on one of the fishing boats." Earlier, I had suggested holding her for a hostage, but Uncle Raymond would have none of it.

"They must go because we don't want Devon and his heirs to have any connection to the castle, particularly if he's still alive. The damn French are romantic, aren't they? They might forget the king and send an army to try to rescue her if she's here."

We dismissed the servants for the night and carried our own food from the cookhouse to the great hall where we and all of our men would eat and sleep while we were here. Everyone was totally exhausted. It had been a long day.

That night we slept soundly in Rougemont's great hall with the gate closed, the drawbridge raised, our weapons close at hand, and a dozen or more men sleeping next to the gate and at entrance to the now-partially-collapsed escape tunnel.

****** *George*

The first thing in the morning, right after we broke our fast with flatbread and morning ale, Uncle Raymond, Richard and I, and an escort of more than twenty heavily armed horse archers followed a horse cart full of Lady Margaret's daughters and their personal bedding, clothes, and chamber pot down to the Exeter quay. When we got there, we put a very unhappy and constantly protesting Lady Margaret on a carefully selected fishing boat and sent her and her daughters off to France.

The weather was good; they should make it.

We stood on the quay next to our horses and watched as the newly-rich three man crew of the little fishing boat raised its sail and headed out of the harbour. As soon as it cleared the harbour entrance we mounted up and rode into Exeter to see if we could buy food and siege supplies for the castle.

The city was unknown to us and we were not certain as to the reception we would receive, but we were not about to leave for Windsor until Rougemont had more than enough siege supplies in hand to hold off an attacking army until a relief force could return and lift the siege. After we visit the market, we intend to stop for a bowl at the ale house nearest the castle, the one run by the retired archer and his wife who spy for us.

****** *George*

Our arrival at the city gates and entrance into the city caused more than a bit of anxiety among the local residents. The city gates were open and no one challenged us as we rode in. Even so, people quickly deserted the streets and some of the merchants began frantically closing their stalls.

The sudden appearance of more than twenty heavily armed men will do that every time.

Things quickly changed when Uncle Raymond opened his pouch and began buying food and firewood. The merchants who had closed their stalls quickly reopened them, and the streets of Exeter were soon once again filled with people going about their daily lives.

Exeter's merchants ended up being quite happy to see us and have our custom; and, without exception, each merchant we spoke with quietly asked us if was really true that the earl's army had been destroyed and the earl killed. The merchants all knew we had won, of course, because survivors of the earl's army had been coming into the city ever since yesterday afternoon, but they didn't know how decisive our victory had been.

Yesterday afternoon? They must have run all the way. It's a good thing we rode all night and went straight into an attack when we arrived.

Each and every one of the merchants was subdued when they heard the earl's army had been destroyed, and looked worried when we admitted that we didn't know if the earl survived. The earl was not, so it seemed, well liked in the city. If half of what we were told was true; the earl's taxes had been high and his treatment of the people unreasonable. Everything we heard about the earl and the city confirmed what we'd been told by our spies, the man and woman we hoped we would be meeting in a few minutes.

The merchants were particularly and understandably concerned, to their credit Richard and I agreed, that many local men in the earl's levies had been killed or wounded. Indeed, by the time we left the market a sizable crowd had gathered around us to inquire about their missing sons and husbands, of which we could tell them nothing.

Some people, we were told, were already walking and riding to the scene of the battle to see if they could find their men and retrieve their bodies. There were great cries and laments when we said we had let the survivors run off and held no prisoners. It meant the missing men were likely dead.

Our coins soon bought almost all the available food and firewood in the market including a number of sheep and beeves. We also ordered and prepaid for much more to be delivered as soon as possible. The elated merchants counted their coins and agreed to unload the food and firewood at the entrance to the drawbridge and go away.

Only when the food deliverers were gone, and no one else was in sight, would the drawbridge would be lowered and our men go out and carry the supplies to the gate which would remain closed. Then the drawbridge would be raised and the gate opened so the supplies could be safely carried inside the bailey—and all the time there would be a force of archers on the battlements ready to push out arrows at anyone who tried to enter.

The castle's servants would follow the same process when they came to work each day—and never in the months and years ahead would the drawbridge be down and the gate open at the same time.

We've been involved in sieges before, and Uncle Thomas spent long hours in his school talking about them; no enemies of ours were going to get the archers out of Rougemont without a prolonged siege and serious fighting that would cost our enemies most dearly.

****** *George*

From the market we went to visit the alehouse where we hoped to find the old archer and his wife who are our spies. None of us had been here before but we had a good idea of where it was located and found it easily. There was a picture of a bull and a bear painted on the wall next to the alehouse's low and narrow entry door.

We dismounted, hobbled our horses, and everyone entered. I had to bend my neck to get my head low enough to enter the Bull and Bear. Once again our arrival caused fear and consternation.

There were three or four men sitting together with bowls in front of them. They looked up and their eyes widened as we walked in. The fearful and concerned alewife and her equally anxious husband quickly motioned for their customers to leave by an even smaller rear door. They looked at the anxious alewife and her husband sympathetically and murmured encouragements as they stood up and hurriedly left.

Then, to the surprise and absolute amazement of Richard and the archers, the looks on the faces of the worried couple changed to broad smiles as soon as the last of the four men was out the door and it was shut and barred behind them—they flew into Raymond's arms and he gave them great hugs and friendly cries of endearment. There was no doubt about it and it was instantly clear to every man in the room, these were friends, very good and dear friends.

One of the older archers stood up from the bench where he had just seated himself and cocked his head and squinted as he looked at the alehouse man with a look of disbelief on his face.

"Tom, is that you? It is, isn't it? Well I'll be damned. We all wondered what had happened when you and your wife disappeared so sudden. So we did. By God, it's good to see you alive and doing so well."

"Hoy Fred. Aye, it's me and me mizzus."

What followed was another round of handshakes, back slappings, and happy talk as the smiling alewife began dipping bowls into a barrel and started handing them around to the now immensely pleased and grinning archers.

"Lads," Uncle Raymond called out a few moments later with a hard and serious sound in his voice as he raised his hands up to timbered ceiling of the alehouse, which wasn't hard because it was only three or four inches above his head.

"You're to forget we ever came here and you're never to tell anyone that we ran into old friends; not your best mates nor your wives. You're not to talk to anyone about being here; not ever." Everyone nodded their understanding. Of course they did.

Then we huddled around a small table in the corner and Richard and I listened whilst Tom told Raymond the bad news—several of his regulars were sure they'd seen the Earl of Devon board a fishing boat last night and sail away.

Chapter Nine

It's time to leave.

The relief company of foot archers marched over the drawbridge and into Rougemont's bailey about four hours after sunrise whilst we were still at the market buying supplies and visiting our spies. We returned to find them exhausted but recovering quickly in response to the morning ale, bread, and cheese which had been set out and was waiting for them in anticipation of their arrival.

"A good night's sleep and they'll be as good as new," was how their captain, Jack Saltich, described his company of foot archers.

Jack was known as a steady and dependable man which, of course, was almost certainly why Henry had suggested Jack and his company be given the responsibility of holding Rougemont if there was no need of a siege—and why I decided it was safe to leave and head for Windsor.

Moreover, in addition to Jack's company of about eighty men, Uncle Raymond announced that he would be leaving twenty horse archers at Rougemont under a dependable sergeant to act as Jack's outriders and couriers, as well as pouch of coins to buy supplies. It would be a strong force in a strong castle.

And Rougemont was, indeed, a strong castle. If it was used properly, an army of two thousand men, or even more for that matter, wouldn't be able to retake Rougemont with an assault. It would have to either besiege the castle and starve them out or gull its way in somehow. It would be up to me to decide whether it was safe for me to leave or if I should stay here in Devon to command the castle's defenders and sergeant its preparations to withstand a siege.

Actually, I'd already decided. There was no siege and no enemy in sight, so Richard and I would gallop for Windsor with a dozen or so of the horse archers as soon as we were able to get at least six months of siege supplies into— the castle. I was confident that Jack and his men would be able to hold the castle until we returned even if the Earl of Devon was still alive, even if the French or the barons sent an army to help him recapture it.

Getting in enough supplies, however, was a big "if" despite our initial warm welcome from the Exeter merchants. We'd know soon enough; either the supplies we ordered would be delivered by the merchants or they wouldn't. And what should I do if they weren't?

****** *George*

Uncle Raymond and the horse archers left the next
afternoon for Windsor. He intended, Uncle Raymond told us
as we stood there next to him while he adjusted his saddle, to
ride all night tonight and reach Okehampton tomorrow in
time to spend tomorrow night with his wife, so he can get her
"good advice," before he and his horse archers ride on to join
up with our main army as it marched to Windsor.

Richard and I, on the other hand, would stay behind to
continue buying siege supplies for the castle and organizing
its defence. We're to stay until I decide Rougemont has
enough supplies to withstand a siege of at least six months.
Some of Raymond's horse archers were staying with us in
addition to the twenty who would be staying permanently
with Jack; they were the men who would be riding with me
to Windsor if and when I decide the castle is secure enough
for Richard and me to go.

"Oh George, what do you intend to do with the priests
you're holding, hang them? And why do you suppose we
haven't heard from the prebend in charge of the Devon
diocese?" Those were the last words I heard from Uncle
Raymond as he swung himself into his saddle and prepared
to lead the horse archers on a fast march along the London
road.

I opened my mouth to say something—and then shut it
and shook my head helplessly. I hadn't a clue as to what to
say; I was speechless. Uncle Raymond smiled down at me,
raised his hand to signal his waiting men, and then, whilst I

was standing there pondering his questions, led them out through the bailey gate to begin their long march to Windsor.

The priests and the church? I hadn't given either of them a thought.

****** *George*

Uncle Raymond really got to me with his questions about the two priests and the role of the church both in their foul behaviour and in Devon. Accordingly, after checking to make sure the promised supplies had been arriving, I walked to the gate house where the two prisoners were living and again questioned them for over an hour about their experiences with the priests and their life under Eustace, the monk who had become a pirate.

Afterwards, armed with the additional information and a much better understanding of what the freed prisoners had been doing before Devon arrested them, I took a candle lantern and went down into the dungeon to question the priests once again.

I found the priests alive and filthy from standing in their own piss and shite, but not as shrill and demanding as when I last saw them. To the contrary, they both were hungry and thirsty, and willing to talk, particularly when I suggested I might let them have some water if they told me everything and I found it all to be true.

I didn't say anything about the justice of them suffering exactly what the same privations they had put on their prisoners, and without the torture they had so gleefully inflicted. But I thought about it behind my eyes, yes I did.

The priests were happy to see me and anxious to tell me whatever I wanted to know in order to get water. According to the priests, it was the prebend of Exeter Cathedral and the Devon diocese, a priest by the name of Father Horace, who had received the earl's order for the execution of the sailors and assigned the priests to punish them before they died. The prebend, of course, being the man who captains a cathedral and diocese when they have no bishop to sell indulgences and gobble the prayers in the church talk needed to make them effective.

"We're the ones his excellency usually asks," croaked the big priest agreed. He almost seemed proud at having been selected to torture the prisoners.

"Did he tell you to deny the prisoners food and water and torture them until they died?" I asked.

The little priest answered once again and his answer was chilling.

"It's what we always do," he said with a little smile as if he relished it. The bigger priest nodded. "It's what the church expects.   People who misbehave have to be disciplined, don't they? It's in the bible, isn't it?"

"The prebend o Exeter, Father Horace, knew this, did he?" I asked. "That you were going to deny the earl's prisoners food and water, and torture them until they died? Did he or the earl help you torture them?"

They both agreed that both Father Horace and the earl knew what would happen and assisted in the torturing.

"And the other priests in the diocese, did they know?" I asked.

"Of course," was the answer from both of them. "It's God's will, isn't it?" Then I asked them in Latin which verses in the bible called for the torture of condemned prisoners, or anyone else for that matter. They didn't know. And they didn't even realize that I had begun speaking to them in Latin.

"Did the earl know they would be tortured? Are you sure?" I asked.

"Oh aye. He helped us didn't he? Very religious isn't he?"

"Well," I finally said after a moment of thinking behind my eyes, "you answered my questions so I'll send a guard down with a bowl of water for each of you." Then I inquired about each of the other priests in the Devon diocese and asked if any of them had ever mentioned being uncertain about it being God's Will to torture prisoners.

I walked out of the foul dungeon quite angry and not at all sure what I should do with the priests. Convene the sergeants to sit in a judgement on them? Kill the murderous bastards out of hand, or let the two surviving prisoners do it? But how would Exeter's merchants and people react if they knew we executed them? and what should I do about the prebend and the involvement of the church?

Thinking about so many things behind my eyes made my head ache most hurtful.

My mood brightened considerably when I came back to the great hall after my visit to the dungeon. Whilst I was in the dungeon questioning the priests, a galley had arrived from the Fowey with a full crew of archers at its oars. It was, according to the parchment its captain brought to me from Harold, to be stationed at Exeter for as long as it was needed. Harold had his apprentice sergeant scribe the message and dispatched the galley when a courier arrived telling him we'd taken Rougemont.

The galley's captain was Evan Jones. I knew Evan quite well; he'd been a three-stripe sailing sergeant on a galley that had carried Uncle Thomas to Rome to pay the Pope his share of our take from our passengers' prayer coins. I had sailed with Uncle Thomas as his apprentice sergeant to learn how our annual transfer of the coins to the Pope was accomplished. Evan and I had passed the time playing chess.

Evan and the archers on his galley were unexpected reinforcements and warmly welcomed by everyone. He and his lieutenant had walked up from the Exeter quay with a party of archers from his galley and joined me and Richard and Jack, and Jack's lieutenant, in the great hall for a bowl of ale and some bread and cheese. We also pulled apart and ate three chickens which had been cooked in the cook house and brought to us by the castle servants. They were most tasty.

Much of our meeting was spent reviewing the entire situation, everything from what might be done about the torture priests and the church to what Evan and his men should do and not do if an enemy appeared by land or sailed into Exeter by sea.

When we finished, I made it clear to Evan and everyone else that Jack would be in command of the castle and this part of Devon's lands when Richard and I left for Windsor—which might be as soon as the day after tomorrow if the food and firewood supplies for the castle's siege supplies kept coming in as they had today.

After we finished telling each other what we knew and thought, and I had listened to everyone's opinions, I cobbled together a war party of about twenty horse archers and accompanied Evan and his men back to the quay. This time, instead of walking, Evan and his men rode in a one-horse wain with an archer driving the horse.

We sat on our horses and waited for a moment whilst Evan's galley which was anchored just off the quay was pulled back up to the quay by a long mooring line so they could climb aboard. Then we shouted our farewells as it was pushed off to return to its nearby anchorage, wheeled our horses around, and rode to the cathedral to visit the prebend of the diocese. Richard and Jack came with me. Jack's lieutenant had stayed behind at the castle to make sure the gate was never open at the same time the drawbridge was down and that each was heavily guarded when it was in use.

******

Our ride through the streets of Exeter to the cathedral was noticed, but mostly ignored, by the people of the city. There were people and carts in the streets we travelled, and everyone certainly looked at us as we slowly and casually rode our horses towards the cathedral, Exeter's largest and most impressive building except for the nearby castle. But we were riding relaxed, not brandishing weapons or riding with grim determination. As a result, the people in the city's streets and lanes were curious but paid us no great mind as we passed.

When we got to the cathedral, we didn't enter it via its huge front doors; we used the priests' entrance in the rear in order to avoid disturbing anyone who might be praying or confessing. As we dismounted and walked towards the door I reminded Richard not to let the priests know we both spoke Latin.

A man can learn much by listening to what other people say when they think they cannot be understood by those around them. It was something we'd had been learnt in school; I'd found it to be true.

Only Richard, Jack, and I entered and, before we did, we took off our swords and left them in the wain along with our bows. All the rest of our men stayed outside and stood around holding the reins of their horses and casually talking in small and relaxed groups. Several of the men took advantage of the opportunity and pissed up against the cathedral's rear wall.

The three of us walked through the narrow rear door and into a room which had several priests sitting around a splendidly carved wooden table eating and talking. Beyond them, through a partially opened door, we could see the great hall of the cathedral where the people of the city gathered to pray, receive the priests' blessings, and tender their donations. There were a handful of people scattered about kneeling and praying in the semi-darkness.

It was everywhere very quiet and peaceful, and so were we. Somewhere in the background prayers were being chanted. The light that lit the room came into it from openings high up above us in the wall. It was quite dim.

Two priests sitting at the table looked up with surprise as we entered. People, it seemed, did not usually enter through the rear door. One of the priests immediately stood up and came walking towards us with an uncertain and questioning look on his face; the other took a big drink from the wooden bowl he was holding with both hands, and then he too stood up, gave us a nod to acknowledge our presence, and walked out into the cathedral's great hall.

"Hoy brothers. I am Father Pierre, may I help you in some way," the priest said as he approached us and made the sign of the cross to bless us. He had a suspicious and unwelcoming look on his face and spoke in English with a heavy French accent.

"Hoy, Father Pierre," I replied in English with a friendly smile on my face. "I'm George of the Company of Archers in Cornwall and the papal order of the Poor Landless Sailors. It is my men who now hold Rougemont Castle and I am its new constable. I'm here to speak with the prebend. Is he available? I'd like to get his prayers for our success and to arrange for a priest to provide services at the castle for our men."

I spoke quite sincerely and smiled a lot as I made my inquiry.

I was, of course, telling a lie; I wasn't there to speak with the prebend, I was there to either kill him or, much to be preferred, arrest him and a certain Father Francis who also enjoyed torturing people—because, according to the torture priests, they were the two people most likely to help the Earl of Devon escape if he was still alive and be able to tell us where to find him.

Father Pierre's face brightened only slightly at the news. "Oh yes; I'm sure he'll want to talk to you. I'll go fetch him."

The priest immediately walked out into the cathedral's great prayer hall. I quickly whispered some additional instructions to my two fellow archers.

******

A tall and thin ferret-faced priest with white hair and a badly pocked face showing through his grey-flecked beard bustled into the room a few minutes later. He was wearing a particularly fine robe with a fur trim and he had bad teeth. Trailing along right him was a big, burly man and the priest who gone to fetch him. The big man was clearly some kind of guard. He wore a sword.

"God's blessing on you all. I am Father Horace, prebend of the diocese. Father Pierre says you are the new constable at the castle and wish to see me?" The prebend was clearly anxious as he eyed the four of us. He tried to smile as he greeted us, but it came across as forced and unreal. He was clearly nervous and rightly so—we might have come to loot the cathedral or arrest him.

"God's blessing on you, Father Horace. I am George of the company of archers and the new constable of Rougemont Castle. I am here to talk with you about the religious needs of the castle and also, of course, to make a donation for your prayers." I touched the linen pouch hanging from my tunic rope as I told my lie.

We proceeded to speak at length about what it might cost to have a priest permanently at the castle to help the men with their prayers. Father Horace was also interested in knowing about the Order of Poor Landless Sailors and seemed suitably impressed about its good works carrying refugees and pilgrims in the Holy Land and its connection to the Holy Father. I took advantage of the situation to mislead him in case he somehow escaped the fate I had planned for him, by tripling the number of men I said were in the castle "needing prayers and such."

As we talked I suddenly became aware of something strange. The sunlight coming in from openings high in the walls of the room suddenly revealed the room to be full of little pieces of dust or tiny bugs hanging in the air. The air was thick with them and they weren't moving, but only where the sign was shining directly into the room. I'd seen something like this before at times, but never so much. It distracted me for a moment when the prebend asked me about our men. I wondered if the light hatched them. I'll have to ask Uncle Thomas.

"Oh yes, Father Horace, they all speak English."

Hmm. The priests in the Rougemont dungeon didn't mention a guard and the prebend didn't ask me how I came to be the constable or about the two priests we captured. He obviously already knows that the earl is gone and his army destroyed. That's not surprising; the whole city must know by now. But does he know what happened to the earl and his two priests—and does he have a guard because he fears for his life, or is he always just a cautious man?

Chapter Ten

There are problems.

Richard and Jack stepped out of the room and into the great prayer hall when I nodded towards the door. I wanted them gone so Father Horace and I could put our heads together and talk privately about money matters.

I motioned for the two priests to follow them and, after a few moments of indecision and getting a nod of agreement from the prebend, they followed Richard and Jack into the prayer hall. Without saying a word, the guard shook his head and remained when I gestured for him to leave with them.

I shrugged my acceptance of the guard's refusal and once again explained our needs to the prebend as I untied my pouch and reached into it to grab a large handful of coins.

"We need a priest of our own because we have so many men in the castle who have done many bad things and need to buy prayers and indulgences. There are over three hundred of them aren't there?" I said as I began to count coins into a hand that jumped forward and opened to take them.

Then I added, "I've heard of a certain Father Francis from one of the merchants who might do for us as our confessor because he can speak English. Could I meet him?"

Father Horace was clearly still suspicious and uncertain about me, but the feel of the coins being counted into his hand apparently greatly reassured him. His sandals made a strange clip clopping sound on the stone floor as he walked to the door and called out one of the priests in the cathedral's great praying hall to go to the priory and fetch Father Francis. He must be wearing the new sandals with wooden soles that have become so popular at the king's court and among the nobility.

****** *George*

Father Horace and I talked of many things while we waited for Father Francis to join us, including the weather and this year's crops on the church land assigned to support him as the cathedral's prebend—everything but the defeat of the earl's army and the whereabouts of the Earl of Devon

I asked the prebend if he had heard from the earl since his army was defeated, but Father Horace professed to know nothing and not to be very interested in such matters "because watching over the lands and properties of the diocese and caring for the faithful takes all my time."

I don't know what I expected when the priest finally arrived, but Father Francis was a surprise—he was a gaunt and strange-looking man with a look of madness in his eyes and a robe and hair so long and filthy that he might have been a Templar whose knights and sergeants never cleaned themselves in an effort to live as much as possible like Jesus who, being a god, never had to do such things.

My two lieutenants came in behind Father Francis and they shut the door in the face of the priest who'd gone to fetch him. That's when things fell apart even before a word was spoken. It was my fault. I had instructed Richard and Jack to keep everyone else out so we could "talk" privately with Father Francis and the prebend—meaning quietly arresting them and hustling them out the back door and into the waiting wain.

The effort to deny the priest entrance by shutting the door in his face was done too abruptly. It somehow signalled to the churchmen, and even to me, that there was going to be a conflict. The result was inevitable—the guard started to draw his sword and the priests drew away from us and darted their eyes about in a frantic effort to find a way to escape. It was the very thing I was trying to prevent, and it happened.

I had no choice. I leapt on the burly guard like one of our castle cats taking a mouse and shouted "hold the door" as I did.

The burly guard stumbled backward, tripped over his own feet, and went down hard. The hand that had half drawn his sword instinctively let go of it and went behind him to break his fall. I went down on top of him with the point one of my wrist knives pricking him in the throat and the blade of the other cutting into the side of his neck as he twisted—but only a scratch, not deeply.

Why didn't I kill him? Because neither of the torture priests had mentioned him; for all I knew he might be an innocent man merely trying to do his duty and earn bread for his family.

The guard froze when he felt my knives at his throat. I kept them carefully pressed against his neck and throat as I slowly rolled off of him and knelt on the stone floor next to him, all the while keeping them in place.

"Get some of the men in here to help us take them out to the wain," I snapped to Jack as Richard finished pulling the guard's sword from his sheath and held its point at the guard's heart. Jack dropped the wooden bar in place to keep the prayer room door closed and ran to get our men.

I was not in a good mood as I got to my feet. There was shouting in the cathedral's great hall and someone was soon banging on the barred door. My plan for quietly taking the prebend and the priest had gone to hell in a bucket. Little did I know what would happen next to make things even worse.

****** *George*

Our white-faced and trembling prisoners, including the burly guard with the bloody scratch on his neck, were hustled out of the back room of the cathedral at sword point and hurriedly loaded into the wain with an archer sitting on either side of them. The mates of the archers in the wain led their horses, and every archer including me had his longbow strung and in his hand and an arrow nocked.

We didn't get very far. We were clattering down the street towards the city gate nearest the road to London when Father Francis suddenly tried to vault out of the bed of the wain and run to safety. He didn't make it. He was sliced by a least one of his guards' swords as he jumped out of the wain and then hit with several arrows as he began to run.

Father Francis ran less than ten steps before he lurched sideways and bounced off a wall we'd been passing, and collapsed on to the dirt street with a terrified scream. The people on the street going about their everyday affairs saw and heard what happened—and began running every which way in effort to get away from being involved.

Everyone began shouting and talking at the same time including me.

"Get him back in the wain and shut him up," I shouted even before Father Francis finished collapsing on to the street. "Everyone stay mounted."

The archers who had jumped out of the wain to pursue Father Francis picked him up and tossed him back into the wain like a sack of corn. He was gasping like a fish out of water and trying to sit up and talk with blood running out of his mouth as we resumed our trip back to the castle. Except now, instead of sitting between the two archers, he was lying on his side in front of them with the shafts of two arrows sticking out of his back and the point of one of them sticking out of the front of his robe.

The archers who had been sitting on either side of him as guards had embarrassed looks on their faces, thinking that they had failed and their mates had seen them do it. I wasn't so sure; I'd seen the whole thing and I don't think there was any way that they could have known Father Francis would suddenly try to jump out and run. He certainly surprised me.

"Don't feel bad about it, lads," I said loudly to give them a little encouragement and save their reputations as we resumed clattering down the street at any easy amble, "you couldn't have known he was going to make a try at escaping, and you moved fast and got him right away, didn't you? Shite happens; don't worry about it.

"Oh, and no mercies until we get him to the castle and can question him." *If he lives that long.*

On the way back to the castle I decided to keep our terrified and trembling prisoners separate from each other and from the two priests we already had in the dungeon. No sense in letting them talk and agree on the lies they would tell us.

Damn, I made a mistake; I should have separated the first two torture priests as well. And where should I put these three?

****** *George*

Father Francis had gone asleep from his wounds as wounded men often do. He just periodically gasped and mumbled such that I couldn't question him, not even after one of the archers threw a bowl of water on his face to wake him up. So I gave up, left him in the wain with instructions for someone to come get me if he awakened.

While I was waiting for the prebend to awake, I went down into the foul dungeon to once again question the torture priests. I didn't tell them that we had captured the guard and the cathedral's prebend, Father Horace, and almost certainly killed Father Francis.

"I'll give you some water if you tell me everything you know about the guard at the Cathedral named Derek, the smith's son, the big one with the red beard who is Father Horace's guard. Does he also torture prisoners?" I asked the two priests in Rougemont's dungeon.

"Derek? Derek's not a guard. We don't have guards," the big priest croaked through his parched lips. "He just works around the cathedral, doesn't he? Digs graves and such." The little priest nodded his agreement.

"How about torturing people. Did he help you?"

"Of course not. Putting punishments on people who misbehave is not for the likes of men like him; it's what we priests are supposed to do, isn't it?"

The two priests talked and talked, particularly after they were each given a drink of water and promised more if they would tell me everything they knew about Father Horace. How long had they known him? Who had he tortured and where had he done it? His relationship with the earl? Who had appointed him? That sort of thing—the information that might be helpful to know when I questioned Father Horace and made a decision about his future.

By the time I finished questioning them, I knew much more about the torture priests and the prebend being right proper bastards, including the names of some of the men and women they had tortured in recent years and why. Many of them were local people who didn't pay their tithes on time. Others were a couple of franklins who hadn't paid what the earl considered to be enough taxes and merchants who hadn't paid their protection coins to the local hard men who served as the church's collectors.

I also knew two new things—the guard didn't deserve to be punished for anything and the Father Horace was somehow related to the Earl of Devon and hoped to be named as the new archbishop. He was a relative of the earl's wife and often supped with them at Rougemont.

I learned that it was in the Rougemont dungeons that Father Horace and the earl kept their prisoners and tortured them to death "because the cathedral had no proper place where we could do it."

"Give them each a bowl of water and a flatbread." I said to the archers guarding them as I came out of the dungeon holding a candle lantern and walked to the horse stall where Father Horace was chained.

"Well now," I said as I stood in the entrance of the stall and looked at the prebend where he sat in chains with his back up against the back wall. "I've finished my inquiries about you and it's time for us to talk. What is your relationship to the earl; are you a relative of his or his wife?"

I already knew it was his wife; I wanted to know if he was telling me the truth.

What followed was rather predictable. At first Father Horace blustered and threatened. He told me God would punish me because I killed a priest and took others away from doing God's work, and all sorts of blather. He denied he was related to the earl in any way; said he had not seen the earl since he came to pray before he marched away with his army; and denied he had ever tortured or ordered anyone to be tortured. Then he worked himself into a fine rage and once again he threatened me and demanded that he and the two priests I was holding be freed and allowed to return to the cathedral.

Father Horace stopped for a second when he realized that he'd just admitted that he knew the two priests were here at Rougemont, but then he continued to rage and threaten. That lasted until I walked to the nearby smithy and brought back a red hot horseshoe; that's when he changed his mind and decided to talk with me and tell me all he knew.

By the time we finished, he had a painful burn on his hand and I knew much more about the priests and the prebend being right proper bastards, including the names of some of those they had tortured and why. I also knew two new things—the guard didn't deserve to be punished and Father Thomas was related to the Earl of Devon and hoped to be named as the new archbishop. He was a relative of the earl's wife and often supped at Rougemont. It was in the Rougemont dungeons that he and the earl kept their prisoners.

I listened to Father Horace's stories and threats for a while and then, when I was ready to leave, shocked him speechless when I told him, in Latin, that I had talked to the two priests and their prisoners and knew that many of his stories were lies, that he was a disgrace to the church, and that I intended to tell the Holy Father about his torture of people who didn't pay the earl's taxes and other unchristian behaviours the next time I handed the Holy Father the prayer coins collected by the Pope's Order of Poor Landless Sailors.

"You lie. You've never met the Pope and you never will," he called after me and shook his head to show his disbelief as I walked away.

Actually, I did lie; I had no intention of telling the Holy Father anything at all. I'd made up my mind while he was ranting at me. It wouldn't be necessary to tell the Holy Father about him even if I could. The only question was where and when to do what needed to be done with him.

Chapter Eleven

On the road to Windsor.

Two days later I saddled my horse and got ready to ride out of Rougemont bound for Windsor. It was early in the morning and the sun was barely up. Richard and some of the horse archers were riding with me, a dozen men in all, with each of us leading his saddled remount as a supply horse carrying his additional weapons and such.

We intend to make a fast trip and didn't expect trouble along the way. A force the size of ours should be more than enough to deter any barons who might try to collect tolls on the king's roads and other robbers and felons.

It was alright for me to leave to join our main army at Windsor, I decided after talking it over with Richard and Jack and inspecting the castle's larder, because our garrison was so strong and our coins had kept the supplies coming in from the local merchants. As a result, there was now already enough food and firewood in the castle for Jack and his archers to endure a long siege.

Moreover, additional supplies were continuing to arrive in response to our coins despite the kerfluffle at the cathedral; coins, it seems, were much more important to the local merchants and farmers than a handful of missing priests who could gobble prayers in Latin and sell salvation. Water, of course, was no problem because the castle had its own well.

The three priests we were holding for their tortures and murders had been a problem that was quickly solved. They would be going to Cyprus in chains on our next outbound galley. Evan would hold them on his galley in the Exeter harbour until an outbound galley became available.

If they survive the voyage, the three priests would arrive in Cyprus with rowing blisters on their hands and a parchment from me to Yoram explaining who they were and what they had done, and suggesting that they be immediately topped or, even worse for them, sold to the Moors as galley slaves.

We'd already begun putting the story out in Exeter's ale houses and taverns that the three priests had repented and confessed their evil ways, and were on their way to the Holy Land to pray for God's forgiveness and to help save the refugees fleeing from the heathen Saracens. It wasn't true, of course, but it was working, our spies reported, because it was such a good story and could be told most sincerely—the redemption of sinners and so forth.

The fourth priest, Father Francis, the torturer who died of having arrows stuck in him, wouldn't be a problem either. Last night justice was served and he was appropriately buried—we tipped him into the trench behind the keep that served as the castle's shite hole and dug a new one.

****** *George*

Getting to Windsor to join our army suddenly and unexpectedly took on a great importance once we waved our farewells and clattered out over the drawbridge leading our supply horses. And to this very day I don't know why it did. I just suddenly felt that we should hurry and became silently angry behind my eyes for not leaving earlier. There were thirteen us—Richard, me, and eleven horse archers under Sergeant Joseph, a wheelwright's son from Manchester.

Our ride was rapid and totally uneventful until we reached the battlefield where the earl's army had been destroyed. We met the usual traffic on the road before we reached it as well as people returning from the battlefield after searching for their missing loved ones. They usually didn't meet our eyes as we passed them. A few of them muttered and cursed us as we passed.

The battlefield itself was easy to find both by smell and by sight. There were people prowling about among what was left of the bodies trying to find missing men and the great flocks of birds feasting on them flapped away and circled over us until we passed. The bodies of the men and horses had been left where they'd fallen. What was left of them was mostly bad smells and bones. Their bodies were on both sides of the road and had long ago been picked over for anything of value. Even the rags they had been wearing were gone.

It had been a great victory, yet I found the battlefield quite depressing and muttered a few prayers as I rode through it. It seemed to have a similar effect on many of my men, even the most hard of them. We picked up the pace as soon as we reached the battlefield and maintained it until we finished passing through.

We were still passing through the last of the battlefield when it happened. I saw a distraught and ragged young woman sitting off to the left of the road at the edge of the nearby trees with an infant at her breast and her arm around a young child. She had obviously been weeping and looked to be starving and on her last legs. She was the most forlorn person I'd ever seen.

I rode on for several hundred paces. And then, for some reason I couldn't explain, I pulled up my horse and began riding back to her. My men rode on for a while and then they pulled up to wait for me. Richard or Joseph must have called a halt.

"Hoy missus, is everything alright with you?" *What a stupid question. Of course everything is not right with her.*

She raised a feeble hand and her chest heaved, but she didn't say a word. Then she dropped her hand and just looked at me as I dismounted. Finally she spoke.

"My babies," she said in a weak voice. "Could you give them water? Please Lord, we won't trouble you. Just water." *Dear God, what is this?*

"What did you say?" I asked. *Another stupid question; I heard her clear enough.*

She didn't answer, just looked at me.

I dropped my reins and knelt down beside her with my water skin. First I aimed it at mouth of the infant snuggled under her arms and then at the child on her breast, and then held it to her mouth. And then I held her head up with my hand and repeated the rotation over and over again.

Richard rode up and dismounted as I held her head and watered her and her children. He told me later that I had tears in my eyes. Her hair was the colour of my Beth's.

"Bread," I said as I looked up at Richard. "Bring me the food sack on my supply horse."

We were quite a pair, Richard and I. When next I looked up, my men were gathered around and watching as

Richard and I watered little pieces of bread to make them soft and poked them into their desperate mouths, even that of the nursing infant. After a while we began breaking off little pieces of cheese and feeding it to them as well. I could tell that the men wanted to help but didn't know what to do. Someone had returned with my horses which had wandered off because I hadn't bothered to tie them up or hobble them.

"Get my rain skin," I said at one point as the infant at her mother's breast grabbed my finger and held it. Four or five men immediately turned towards my horse to get it and then they all watched carefully as I wrapped it around the three of them. Others had gotten their bread and cheese out and offered it; and several volunteered that they had a skin of wine if it would help. We gave them some of that as well, even the nursing infant.

****** *George*

Richard and I spent the better part of an hour feeding and watering the girl and her little ones and listening to her story when she was recovered enough to tell it. Her husband had been killed in the battle and his stepmother had thrown her and her children out of their hovel as soon as she heard he was dead. She'd walked all this way to try to find his body because she didn't know what else to do.

We left the girl and her children with two volunteers who were instructed to take them to Rougemont as soon as the girl was strong enough to hold her infant and travel riding double. After they dropped them off at the castle and made sure they were being properly treated, the two horse archers were to try to catch up with us on the London road and, if they couldn't which was quite likely since we'd be moving fast, they were to re-join the company in Windsor.

The two volunteers smiled and so did all of the men when I playfully nudged Richard and gave them their orders about the girl and her children.

"Tell the captain of the castle I said that Captain Richard is adopting all three of them, and that he is to see that they are well fed and have a hovel, bedding, and clothes that will keep them warm and dry. Also tell him I said he is to find a place for the girl to work in the castle, perhaps in the kitchen or fletching arrows. She can keep my rain skin; she may need it on the ride to Rougemont and after she gets there."

All of the rough and tough horse archers approved of my orders; I could sense it as we mounted our horses even though no one said a word. We'd all somehow been moved by the plight of the girl and her children. The bodies and the suffering people we'd encountered had somehow changed us.

Later that day, the sun was just finishing its daily move over England as we rode past the cart path that leads up to Okehampton's drawbridge and gate; we didn't stop.

Chapter Twelve

William on the road.

We could see the thatched roof hovels of Staines ahead of us when we began marching right through the middle of the barons' army. Great numbers of scattered tents and temporary shelters were scattered all about on either side of the London Road. Some of the tents had banners hanging from poles in front of them and women and children were everywhere. This was the barons' army and we knew it; we had long ago gotten word as to its location on the London Road both from Thomas and from our couriers carrying messages between Windsor and Cornwall.

I had talked to Henry and Raymond and we decided to show our confidence, flaunt it actually, by riding and marching right through the baron's camp. We didn't slow down and we made quite an appearance as we marched right through the camp to the beat of each company's rowing drum. Raymond's horse archers came first and then Henry's foot archers. There were no stragglers; those of our men who were footsore were riding on top of the supplies and equipment in our wains.

The barons almost certainly knew we would be coming to Windsor to support the king and probably assumed we would bypass their camp by marching around it. In any event, we didn't march around it; we stayed on the road and marched right through it. The barons may have known we were coming but they obviously had not bothered to inform their men. The common soldiers and their women were truly surprised and many rushed to the road and called out questions as to who we might be and where we were going.

As you might imagine, we were on high alert as we passed through the barons' camp. We marched tightly closed up and ready to move instantly into a defensive fighting position. I was riding at the very front of the men on foot and Henry at the very rear. Raymond and his horse archers led the way.

We had marched through their camp and were long gone out the other side before the barons could gather and decide whether or not to oppose us. As you might imagine, we made sure there were no stragglers and the company captains were prepared to move their men into a fighting formation on a moment's notice.

It appeared to be reckless, but it wasn't. We had outriders far out in front of us and would have known early-on if the barons had gathered their men into a fighting formation to oppose our passage. I don't know what we would have done if they had stood to arms and tried to block us—probably marched around them in order to avoid a fight, or at least tried.

****** *William*

My nine companies of foot archers were footsore by the time we reached Windsor. The tenth company which had been Exeter had caught up with us by holding on to the stirrups of Raymond's riders. Its men were totally exhausted. Many of its men and some of my original nine had been reduced to riding on top of their supply wains by the time Henry and I led them and Raymond's horse archers into a meadow near Windsor and told them to pitch their tents.

Despite everyone's exhaustion, we made quite an appearance as we marched in to the beat of each company's rowing drums with our men bellowing out the chants and songs that somehow made long marches more bearable.

Peter and his seven companies of foot archers were not waiting for us, but my brother Thomas soon appeared riding a horse he had somehow acquired during his stay at Windsor to attend the peace conference. He'd been staying at the local parish church with the vicar and his family whilst attending the council charged with writing an agreement for the king and barons.

Thomas immediately rode out to join us. He had gotten word we were approaching from one of the king's couriers who had galloped past us earlier this morning on his way to Windsor. The good news, said Thomas, was that the king had been getting anxious about our arrival and this will placate him; the bad news was that Thomas had heard nothing about Peter and the seven companies of foot archers coming to London from Restormel aboard their galleys.

My brother Thomas may not have known anything about Peter and his men, but he certainly was the bearer of some good family news which he could hardly wait to tell me—I'm a father again according to a parchment that just came in from Helen. George has a new brother out of Tori despite my age. It was quite surprising what with me already being a grandfather three times over out of George's Beth and Becky.

Tori is doing well, according to Helen, and I've finally got both an heir and a spare to keep the family going.

Robert, for that is what he'll be named, was born a few days after we marched out of Restormel, according to the parchment Thomas received last week. The captain of a Scottish cog brought it to our London post and they couriered it to Thomas. The captain got it when he called in at Fowey Village to exchange his cargo of Scottish charcoal for a cargo of roughly smelted tin from one of the king's mines in Cornwall.

The parchment from Helen had been scribed for her by Angelo Priestly, the former priest who puts the learning on the boys in Thomas's school when Thomas is away. It reported that young Robert is doing well with ten fingers and toes, a loud voice, and normal shite, all of which absolutely delighted Tori and Helen. Tori and Helen don't know it yet, but he'll be baptized as Robert, Robert Courtenay, as soon as Thomas and I return to Cornwall and Thomas can pray at him with the proper words.

Yes, I told Thomas about my decision to begin naming myself as a Courtenay; he approved.

"We'll fiddle the Okehampton parish records to make George and young Robert Courtenay lords just as soon as I get back there and can sharpen a quill."

****** *William*

My brother Thomas wasn't the only person who knew one of our archer armies was approaching Windsor. William Marshal and several of the other leaders of the king's army had been alerted to our arrival and were watching from a hill overlooking the pasture land where the archers and I would camp. They were distressed by the unexpectedly small number of men they counted but impressed by how they arrived with their drums beating. They could hardly believe it.

"Walking together is nothing," Lord Vernon of Sunderland finally said rather dismissively. "There are not anywhere near three thousand of them, and they have no knights to lead them into battle and no armour to protect them when they fight."

"No, it's the future," said Marshal quietly as he continued watching. "And we'd be fools to think otherwise."

The king's men, knights every one of them, stayed on the hill and watched for a while as the archers from Cornwall pitched their tents in some kind of squared pattern surrounding their horses and wains. Then they rode back to Windsor Castle to report to the king. They didn't pay any attention to the serf who was arriving to plough the nearby field with a wooden plough pulled by a pair of oxen.

"The archers from Cornwall have arrived, Your Majesty. There are only about a thousand of them, not the three thousand we expected, but they look fearsome nonetheless. It's a good thing we employed them instead of the barons," Sir William told the king. The others disagreed.

"Nonsense, Sir William; they're just common farmers without a single knight to lead them," was Lord Vernon's response. "That's why they've never been paid to fight France like all the other mercenary companies."

"Well then," said the king with a great smile. "We'll send them a man to tell them what to do—you Lord Vernon." Marshal frowned and started to say something. But then he held his tongue.

"And send for the Bishop of Cornwall," the king ordered. "He promised us three thousand men."

******

A totally different meeting occurred some hours later in the barons' camp at Staines. The ragged ploughman had changed back into his regular clothes and was reporting to Robert Fitzwalter and a dozen or so barons gathered in front of a large tent in the barons' camp. He was one of FitzWalter's most trusted sergeants.

"There's nothing to worry about," the sergeant told them. "There are only a little over a thousand of them of whom about one hundred and fifty are mounted. But here's the thing—I didn't see a knight among them or anyone wearing armour. And not a single tent has a banner. They're leaderless."

He was surprised when the disgusted and angry barons rounded on him for reporting what they already knew from watching incredulously as the archers from Cornwall marched right through their camp. What followed was a dispute that got more than a little heated at times.

Fitzwalter was angry that the archers had been ignored as they marched on the road that passed right through their camp. He wanted to attack the archers immediately "to avenge the insult and show the king we have the upper hand." He argued that destroying the archers would make the king more likely to accept the terms they were proposing.

Others of the barons were not so sure; some wanted to wait for the Earl of Devon and his men to arrive and for the return of the barons who had temporarily returned to their fiefs to make sure that this year's crops were properly planted and cared for. A significant number wanted to give Langton and the peace process more time; they wanted lower taxes and their rights, but were not keen to take a chance on getting killed or wounded if it could be avoided.

"We have more than enough men," FitzWalter shouted. "We'll ride right over them." Some of the barons agreed; others did not. The argument got hot when FitzWalter began to question the bravery and honour of those who were not willing to follow him.

In the end, the cooler heads prevailed and FitzWalter backed off when he realized he was in danger of losing some of his followers. A compromise was reached; those who wanted to attack the archers' camp would follow FitzWalter and do so; those who thought it best to wait, would not. That way, they could all claim that the attack was a personal matter between FitzWalter and his friends caused by the archers stealing horses as they marched through their camp and had nothing to do with their dispute with the king.

"After all," said one the men who had decided not to participate and not yet declared himself, "we've seen them up close and know there aren't as many of them as we'd heard there would be and they have no knights to lead them. There will be more fear of our army from the king and his supporters and our position will be strengthened if it only takes a few of our men to defeat their reinforcements."

He didn't mention that he lived near Brereton and had heard rumours years ago about the fate of a band of knights who attacked a company of archers from Cornwall. It might, he thought, be much more difficult than his friends thought. Well, come to think of it, they weren't really his friends and he would enjoy watching.

Chapter Thirteen

The king gets the news.

My meeting with the king was anything but cordial when I returned from the archers' camp that afternoon. He had a sour look on his face when he walked up to me with his courtiers following and looking similarly displeased. The source of his displeasure was soon apparent; William Marshal had reported that scarcely a thousand men had arrived from Cornwall instead of the three thousand we had contracted to provide.

I immediately proceeded to clarify matters.

"Oh no, Your Majesty, please allow me to put your concerns to rest. I am happy to report that the archers and sailors who arrived under the command of the Earl of Cornwall himself, who is your most loyal subject by the way, are only a small part of the many thousands who are coming. Many more are coming by sea to London and have already boarded their galleys and are at this very moment sailing to London from Cornwall. They should arrive any day now. *I hope.*

"Moreover, I have just spoken with the Earl of Cornwall and I have the most splendid news: God is surely on your side, for the archers and sailors of Cornwall, the ones who are just now arriving, met the army of your great enemy, the traitorous Earl of Devon, on the road as it was marching to join the traitors assembling here in opposition to you—and so soundly trapped and destroyed it that Devon's army no longer exists.

"Many hundreds of your worst enemies have fallen, Your Majesty, albeit at great cost to the archers and sailors of Cornwall who have just arrived and are setting up their camp just west of here. It was a great and important victory for you; God is truly on your side."

The wonderful news of his supporters' great and unexpected victory truly stunned the king and his court. King John's face went from an angry scowl as he thought about the small number of archers who had arrived to a great smile when he discovered God was still on his side. The courtiers, of course, faithfully copied his joy.

"We must go in the morning to congratulate our most loyal and esteemed subject, the Earl of Cornwall and his men," the king announced as he rubbed his hands together with great glee as his courtiers applauded his decision and assured each other that God was truly on the side of their beloved king.

Thomas's thinking behind his eyes was racing as he smiled and nodded his pleasure at the king's announcement. *I need to quickly inform William that his army suffered great losses in winning its battle with Devon. It will give us a splendid excuse for bringing fewer than three thousand men to the king's meeting with the barons.*

****** *William*

"We engaged the Earl of Devon's army on the London Road as it passed through a wood on its way to join the traitors at Staines, Your Majesty," I said to the king as he listened intently with his courtiers standing behind him. They too were listening intently and nodding sagely.

At Thomas's suggestion, my men were standing in front of their tents with their longbows and long-handled bladed pikes out of sight. Those with swords were showing them.

"The fighting was fierce and we lost many men killed, Your Majesty, every one of them a loyal subject of yours. Even more of my men were wounded and are now being barbered at Okehampton. But our great losses were worth it, because we totally and completely destroyed Devon's entire army.

"The earl's body was not found among the many dead, so he may have abandoned his men and run. But it makes no difference if he shows up in England again despite his disgraceful conduct, his army has been completely destroyed and will never come against you again, especially since his lands are now held by the men of Cornwall who are loyal to you in every way."

Loyal to the likes of you? Such ox shite. But it's what the king wanted to hear.

******

The king had intended to stay and "honour you for your victory, my dear earl" by inspecting the archers and sailors of Cornwall. But he quickly changed his mind and didn't stay to inspect them when one of his men who had been watching the barons' camp came galloping in with some surprising news—part or all of the army of the barons camped at Staines was on the move without their baggage and appeared to be coming towards our camp and Windsor as a war party.

King John and his courtiers mounted their horses and left quickly to return to the safety of Windsor Castle, and rightly so—the barons might be abandoning negotiations and making their long-threatened attack against the king to remove him. If that's what was happening, it was unexpected and the barons had achieved total surprise. All anyone knew for sure was that some or all of the barons' army was on the move as a war party without its baggage.

William Marshal and I had a brief, but important, conversation before he ran to mount his horse and catch up with the king.

"Can you hold them until I can gather some reinforcements to support you? Marshal asked. "Or would it be better to fold your tents and either pull back or march to join us inside Windsor?"

"Oh, I think we can hold them if we have to fight, Sir William. Reinforcements would be appreciated, of course, if they aren't needed elsewhere and can get here in time; but we'll be staying here with or without them. As you can see, this is a particularly good position if we have to fight."

Henry was standing next to me and nodded his agreement. He had already told me he thought this was as good a place as any for us to fight, and better than most since we'd have time to prepare our defences. Moving into Windsor Castle was an option, of course, but we'd help eat up its siege supplies and be under the command of the king who might misuse us in a poorly organized sally.

I sent Thomas riding off to follow the king and his courtiers to find out what he could about the intentions of the barons' army and what it meant. Were they coming to attack us or the king? Did it mean the end of the negotiations?

****** *Henry*

William and I and our captains were well into our preparations to meet the barons' army coming towards us when a self-important someone called Lord Vernon rode up with some of his knights and tried to take command of the archers "at the request of the king in order that you better fight the king's enemies who are approaching." It was the middle of the afternoon.

"We need to discuss it privately," a very surprised William told his esteemed new commander. He promptly took Lord Vernon by the elbow and steered him into a nearby tent.

A few minutes later William emerged from the tent and announced to Lord Vernon's astonished knights that there had been a terrible accident and Lord Vernon was dead. They barely had time to carry his body from the field before we began to see the first signs of the approaching army that was coming towards us. The barons' men were beginning to gather on a hillside about a twenty minute walk to the east of our camp.

***** *Henry*

Later that afternoon, a little before dusk, we watched as two riders came towards us from the barons' army. To our astonishment, it was a herald, a foppish Frenchman if you can believe it, of the type one usually finds presiding over knightly tournaments. He was riding towards us on a splendidly caparisoned horse with a man riding behind him on a lesser horse and making loud noises to announce their arrival by blowing on some kind of horn.

William, Raymond and I walked a few feet down the hill to see what he wanted; not far enough to put ourselves at risk, but enough to identify ourselves as the men to whom he should speak.

"Bon jour, milords," the man greeted us in French as he rode forward with his hand raised in a peaceful greeting and looked down at us.

"I am Pierre de Lagard, a herald." He said it as he smiled and bowed down towards us from his saddle.

"I am come to see if I can reconcile you with Lord FitzWalter who commands the men on the hill across the way and, if I cannot reconcile you, to seek your agreement as how your two armies should meet in battle and how the battle should be named. May I know your names and titles?"

William answered in English which the horn blowing man had to translate. He'd obviously been chosen for that purpose since he made the most terrible of braying noises with his horn.

"My name is William, that man is named Henry and that man is named Raymond," William said as he pointed to himself and then to Raymond and me. "We are all three archer captains and members of the Pope's Order of Poor Landless Sailors. Presently we are serving in a company of archers in the employment of King John of England."

What William didn't mention was that he spoke French quite fluently and that he was the Earl of Cornwall and the commander of both our order and the company of archers.

"We are surprised that someone such as Lord FitzWalter would be so offended by our presence as to wish to do battle with us," William added as Raymond and I nodded in agreement. "If he does attack us, we will, of course, defend ourselves rather than fold our tents and leave."

"Am I correct, Sir Pierre," William continued most respectfully, "that it is your sworn duty as a herald to tell those who wish to fight us exactly what we say, and not withhold any of our words and thoughts from them?"

When the herald responded with "Oui, most certainly" and nodded, William told him more about who we were and what he thought about FitzWalter and his men.

"Most of us camped here are free men and archers from the company of archers whose home is in Cornwall. Accordingly, since we are free men, we will make no agreements with Lord FitzWalter and his noble friends—because they are well known to be disagreeable cowards who send their village levies to fight in their place and are afraid to ride their horses in battle or lead their men in battle, probably so their men won't see them pissing in their pants when they run away."

William was baiting them right fine, wasn't he?

"As for a name if we fight, we think *The Battle of the Cowardly Knights* is the only name appropriate."

The herald was taken aback by William's answers. It was clearly not the response he had expected.

"Surely you jest, monsieur? A battle is a serious matter whether it be between two men or many hundreds." The herald became quite huffy. "I cannot say such things to the English knights."

"Of course you can. You must; it's your duty as a herald, unless, of course, you have weak blood because you are French and French heralds are afraid to tell even the most cowardly of English nobles what real fighting men such as the archers say about them."

William leaned forward and continued his explanation with the horn blower rapidly translating his words as William looked up at the herald and spoke them.

"Look here, de Lagard. You are absolutely correct that battles are serious matters; but a fight against poorly armed villagers sent into battle by barons who are too cowardly to fight as knights on horseback does no honour to the company of archers, and it certainly doesn't deserve to be named a battle.

"So, if you are not a French coward, I expect you to tell FitzWalter and his cowardly knights that I said to turn around and go home before we set our dogs and women on them and take their horses and shite-filled armour."

And with that, the three of us turned around and walked up the little hill to where our men were building cooking fires and getting ready to eat.

"Well, do you think my insults will work, Henry?" William asked me as Raymond listened intently.

"We'll know in the morning, William," I replied. "They will if the herald is an honest man and he tells FitzWalter and his friends what you said about them. Unfortunately, he is French so we can't be sure."

Chapter Fourteen

We are attacked.

The sun was just starting to go down and there was the smell of rain in the air. The barons' army was just starting to put up its tents on a hill across the way and light its cooking fires. There seemed to be fewer of them than I would have expected—no more than a couple of thousand of whom fewer than two hundred appeared to be mounted. We would be barely outnumbered by two to one if no more arrived.

We were pleasantly surprised at the relatively small number of men who apparently intended to attack us. Thomas had told us that the barons' army had about four thousand men in its camp at the moment. Where were the rest of them? Could they be circling around to fall on our rear after the fighting begins? Had they gone home to make sure their fields were planted?

"It's a pity," I said to Henry, "that our men have not been learnt to make night attacks. That lot over there look vulnerable. Perhaps night attacks are something we should consider practicing in the future?"

"I could take some men over there later tonight and drop some arrows on their camp, if you'd like." Henry made the offer as he nodded his head in agreement with my question about our men being learnt to make night attacks.

I thought about his suggestion, and didn't agree. "No, it's best to let the barons make the first move. This could be an effort to gull us into moving first so we are responsible for ending the peace talks."

It rained most of the night, but the men stayed dry in their tents and the sky cleared by the first light of dawn. There were great puffy white clouds in the sky as my lieutenants and I broke our fast with our men. We could make out activity in the barons' camp across the way. This morning's bread and ale seemed uncommonly good for some reason.

Raymond and his men had already eaten and rode out of camp after the sun arrived. Some of them would act as watchers in our rear in case the rest of the barons' army tried to surprise us; the rest to fight as archers on horseback and keep pressure on the barons' men across the way. Before they rode out of camp they distributed the bladed pikes they carried on their supply horses to the foot archers. There were enough to give us an extra line of pikes across most of our battle front.

Nothing happened for several hours during which Henry and I roamed through our lines and made sure the archers were ready and each of the captains knew what he was to do and where he was to lead his men under various circumstances depending how the fighting developed.

Finally, after a couple of hours, there was movement in the barons' camp and a great and seemingly disorganized mass of men began slowly moving towards us. The good news was that the mounted men seemed to be leading them instead of following them. Perhaps my insults had been effective.

I decided to walk through our lines again to make sure our men were ready. Our horses and wains had already been taken to the rear. Henry came with me to help conduct yet another of the endless inspections that were an archer's lot.

Henry and I walked through our lines joking with our men whilst carrying our bows and a quiver of arrows slung over our backs. Struggling along behind us were our apprentices weighed down with their own longbows, our swords and shields, and all the extra quivers they could carry. They were there to make it clear to our men that we would be standing with them in the coming fight.

We briefly paused at each company to make sure, once again, that its captain and lieutenant knew what to do and where to lead his men if there was a breakthrough into our lines or an attack materialized from the rear or side of our formation. They did. And their sergeants and men standing nearby overheard us and were confident.

****** *Willam*

Henry and I and our captains were standing out in front of our battle lines as the barons' army began to form up on the hillside opposite us; our men were standing at rest in their lines behind us. Our archers and their auxiliaries were as ready to fight as we could get them.

We watched as the barons' mob began to spread out in a line of many little armies with each of the nobles and his knights in front with the noble's banner and each of the noble's foot soldiers massed haphazardly behind him.

"Oh what fools," Henry said under his breath.

"You're right about that," I said as I raised my left arm high over my head and the captains and lieutenants in front of their companies on either side of me immediately copied men and raised theirs. The barons were forming up their men as they would if they were fighting the French and each other—and in doing so they were well within the killing range of our longbows.

The raising of my right hand and those of their captains and lieutenants caused our archers to nock their arrows, hold their bowstrings tight against their chests, and take note of a specific distant target. A moment later I dropped my hand and shouted in my loudest voice.

"Push" … "Push" … "Push."

So did the captains and lieutenants. And their shouts were instantly repeated by their sergeants and chosen men.

Within an instant, almost one thousand of the best archers in the world began launching arrows out their longbows as fast as possible with great grunts and outward pushing thrusts of their bows to give their arrows maximum distance and power. We were using our "longs" for maximum distance; we'd switch to our armour-piercing "heavies" with their weighted shafts and slender iron tips when the knights got closer.

The sky was immediately full of a great swishing storm of arrows and each archer's second and third arrows were already in the air by the time Henry and I and the company captains stepped back into the ranks to add our arrows to the deadly storm that began falling on the barons' men and their horses.

Confusion and chaos instantly reigned in the barons' ranks as screaming men and horses bolted and ran in every direction. Those who hadn't yet been hit often tripped or were knocked over by those who'd already been killed or wounded, and were then hit themselves whilst they were on the ground or trying to recover their balance.

The leader of the barons' army attacking the archers, Robert FitzWalter of Essex, was among the very first to go down. The archers had been learnt many times to go for those of the enemy who appeared to be their leaders wherever possible—and FitzWalter was on horseback next to a big banner in the centre of the line. As a result, he and his horse took multiple hits from the very first flight of arrows and more from those that followed.

FitzWalter's wounded horse bolted and staggered before it fell and knocked down three or four of the unarmoured men on foot who had been standing behind him and to his right. The unprotected men never got up as the hailstorm of arrows directed at FitzWalter and the knights near him fell on them as well.

FitzWalter was hit by numerous arrows but his armour and helmet saved him because the archers were pushing out "longs" instead of armour piercing "heavies. He was helped to the rear and ran for the rear with an arrow through his arm, a badly punctured cheek and a sliced tongue, and a broken finger that had somehow resulted when someone's horse stepped on his hand while he was on the ground after being thrown by his dying horse.

Others of the knights and nobles were not so lucky. Within seconds the ground was strewn with dead and wounded men and horses. And the arrows kept coming out of the sky like the sheets of water of a drenching rain.

Almost all of the knights and their armour-wearing squires and sergeants put their spurs to their horses and instinctively attempted to escape the storm. Some of them made the mistake of trying to escape by riding towards our lines. The archers, as they'd been learnt, concentrated their arrows on them.

None of the riders made it through the pointed stakes in front of our lines to reach our four lines of pike men before they or their horses were hit and went down. Those such as FitzWalter who rode or ran in the other direction were more likely to successfully escape.

It was over almost as soon as it began. There were fleeing horsemen and running foot soldiers going in every direction except towards our lines. Raymond and his men, to their great disgust and a few exceptions, let them go as I had ordered at my brother's suggestion.

Why? Because Thomas said he knew the king would surely excuse us killing anyone who attacked us; he wasn't sure, however, how the king would respond if we rode down and killed men fleeing after they'd been defeated and thrown down their weapons. Some new tournament fad called chivalry was spreading through knights and nobility and the king seemed to be taken with it.

Thomas and I didn't know the king that well at the time, did we? Now we know he was very much like his brother, Richard; had he been asked, he would have encouraged us to kill them all.

****** *Henry*

Sir William Marshal appeared with a troop of forty mounted knights and armour-wearing sergeants of the king's guards long after the brief battle was over. By the time they arrived we had already finished relieving our dead and wounded enemies of their weapons and clothes and providing them with the necessary "mercies" and barbering as good soldiers always do for each other when circumstances permit.

Marshal and the forty guardsmen were our promised "reinforcements" even though the king had obviously not sent them out to join us until after the battle was over.

For years afterwards, usually when we were in the midst of enjoying particularly fine bowls of ale, William and I would wonder if Sir William would have brought them to us at that moment, in time to join the fight, if FitzWalter had delayed his attack until the next day.

We never heard from the herald again or ever heard his name mentioned.

****** *Thomas*

After the battle, whilst the king was still chortling and laughing about the barons' latest defeat at the hands of the archers, I explained to him and to William Marshal what had happened to Lord Vernon.

"It was whilst he was talking about how best to defeat your approaching enemies that poor Lord Vernon suffered a most unfortunate accident, Your Majesty. He tripped on a slippery patch of grass on the hillside where the archers were waiting and somehow fell on the knife he had in his belt." *At least twice in his neck.*

The king was quite understanding and not at all distressed, perhaps because the archers' victory over FitzWalter's men had greatly weakened his enemies and the barons' wounded had revealed divisions in the barons' camp. He assured me he'd pray for Lord Vernon's soul and for the souls of all the archers who fell; I assured him that God would appreciate his generosity. His courtiers, of course, nodded and agreed with us both.

Chapter Fifteen

Peter arrives with his archers.

The first of the galleys carrying Peter and his seven companies of archers reached the London quay where our cogs and galleys usually tie up on a surprisingly warm Tuesday afternoon. The quay was just downstream from the newly finished bridge across the Thames and the closest quay to where the company's London shipping post was located just inside the city wall.

The sun was shining as the galley bumped up against the quay and the mooring lines were thrown to a couple of ragged wharfies. Birds were wheeling and swooping overhead in hopes of a meal to supplement the dead fish and other things that sometimes mysteriously showed up in the river. All along the river people were fishing from the riverbank and from little dinghies and rafts moored along it.

The arrival of Peter's first galley ignited a great flurry of activity as soon the many watchers waiting on the quay realized it was carrying a large number of archers. The usual merchants and women began converging on our moorage seeking custom, and the men of our London post, who had been anxiously waiting on the quay for days, immediately sent a courier galloping to our camp near Windsor to announce its arrival, and another to Oxford to inform Bishop Thomas.

And they weren't the only ones who responded. Several men who had been lounging about near the quay for days suddenly rushed away for reasons known only to them. Little wonder in that—London's various fortresses and the bridge were held by men from the barons' army with the assistance of a substantial contingent of French knights sent by Louis, the crown prince of France. London's strongholds had been taken over by the French when the king withdrew his men from London in order to reinforce Windsor Castle. They would be tremendously interested in the arrival of additional soldiers for one side or the other and would want to be quickly informed.

Much of the barons' army itself, however, was still at Staines barbering its wounds after its losses in a brief battle with the newly arrived archers near Windsor; and the king was safely inside the massive walls of Windsor Castle. They too would all be tremendously interested in the arrival of additional soldiers for one side or the other and would want to be quickly informed.

Instead of mooring at the quay and making for the nearby White Horse tavern for an arrival bowl of juniper brew, the galley's captain was immediately told by the hastily summoned post sergeant that he was to float down to the entrance to the Pool on the lower reaches of the Thames and hold the rest of the archer-carrying galleys there so Peter's army could all arrive together as a single fighting force.

The post sergeant was looking over his should as he relayed William's order and hurriedly described the uncertain local situation to the galley's captain. The post sergeant was a nervous man and expected to see a charging wave of French troops every time he looked around.

By the time the post sergeant finished his brief explanation, the surprised and increasingly anxious galley captain was only too glad to cast off his mooring lines and move away from the quay. He immediately ordered his galley to head back downstream and his archers to break out their weapons and prepare to repel boarders.

In fact, neither the barons' men nor the French had attempted, at least not so far, to in any way interfere with the archers' shipping post or to prevent its archers or the citizens of London from using the city gate nearest the quay. Even so, as you might imagine, the men of our post were constantly on high alert with its reinforced outer door double barred.

Its anxious sergeant had taken no chances; he'd already sent his wife and children to safety in Cornwall, laid in more siege supplies and water, and made three inspections of his post's escape tunnel.

****** *William*

We got word that the first of Peter's galleys had arrived in the Thames both from the post sergeant's courier and also from Thomas who hurried to our camp from Oxford with the same report. It was a great relief to learn that the galleys from Restormel were beginning to arrive. They must have been delayed by bad weather and unfavourable winds in the Channel.

Peter didn't know about the attack on our camp and that open warfare had broken out. There was no time to lose; he needed to be warned that he might well be attacked. That evening, as soon as it got dark, I left Henry in command of the camp and used three narrow barges to float down the Thames with an entire galley company of archers to meet Peter's galleys on the lower Thames.

It was my intention to meet Peter's arriving galleys, and hold them together offshore until they all arrived, and then unload the archer companies they were carrying, and march all of them up to Windsor at the same time. That way the archer companies could stand together as a single fighting force if they were attacked by the barons' men and the French knights who were holding the city—it wouldn't at all do to have each of the galleys arrive independently at the quay nearest our post, or anywhere else for that matter, and discharge its archers so that they could be picked off one by one by the French and rebel forces holding the city.

Ideally, of course, we would just row the galleys up the Thames to Windsor. But we couldn't do that for several reasons—for one, we'd never before taken our galleys past the bridge and didn't know how deep the Thames was in the stretch of the river we'd have to travel.

More importantly, we couldn't row our way up the river even if it was deep enough because the masts of our galleys were too high to pass under the London Bridge unless the drawbridge in the middle span of the bridge was raised by the barons' men who held the bridge, both as our galleys went up the river carrying our army and then again as they came back down the river after unloading our men; it was an unlikely prospect.

"There is no doubt about it," I told Henry and Thomas. "Peter's companies are going to have to march to Windsor from wherever they land on the Thames if they are to join the king's army in time to accompany him to the meeting at Runnymede."

The need to march Peter's army to Windsor was something I should have thought of earlier. In hindsight, it would have been better if we had all stayed together after defeating Devon and marched to Windsor as one large army.

****** *William*

Henry and I agreed that Peter need to be informed of the very real possibility of an attack on the archers he was bringing to Windsor; and I resolved to do it myself so I could lead his army to Windsor. I initially thought about rowing down the Thames in a dinghy to meet him. Henry was appalled at the idea and wouldn't hear of it; he insisted that nothing short of an entire company should go with me in case I was intercepted and had to fight my way clear.

In the end, I had to agree with Henry. So he and I divided Andrew Small's company such that about thirty archers and all their weapons and extra bales of arrows were in each of the three narrow barges we quickly hired from the local watermen based along the Thames near Windsor. We did so without telling the barge owners what we intended to do, only that we would need their barges for as long as a week to carry cargo.

Andrew's archers waited until after it got dark to board their assigned barges. The carried with them their rain skins, five days of cheese and bread, and all of their bladed pikes, stakes, tents, and arrow bales. They would almost certainly need their rain skins and tents in the near future being as they were England; hopefully they would join Peter's arriving archers and they'd all march together to Windsor without ever having to use their weapons.

It was our intention for the three narrow barges to float down the Thames together that night in the dark. In the event the barges got separated, each would continue alone down the Thames and we would rendezvous tomorrow morning in the Lower Pool of the river where, so we hoped, we would find our galleys waiting.

I myself led the way in the first barge with Andrew as my number two commanding the second barge and his lieutenant, the third; Henry would remain to command the archers already in our camp and Thomas would return to Oxford and re-join the peace council.

Most importantly, neither Thomas nor anyone else would not report the imminent arrival of Peter's army of archers to the king—we did not want the barons' spies among the king's courtiers and elsewhere to alert the barons and French in time for them to sally out of London to meet them.

******

We waited until dark fell before we boarded Andrew Small's archers on the barges and pushed off. Waiting until dark was a reasonable thing to do because we wanted to avoid anyone knowing we were going down the Thames. Similarly, the men were forbidden to talk or move about except for a couple of men crouching at the front and sides of the barge to help the bargees push us off with the butt ends of the bargees extra poles if we started to be stranded or bumped up against a quay or another boat or barge in the night.

It quickly became a quiet and peaceful voyage. Many of the archers ended up falling asleep, lulled by the sounds of the night and the gentle swaying motion of the barge.

—Each of the narrow barges was a shapeless dark blob on the water and almost immediately lost sight of the others when the faint moonlight was obscured by a passing cloud. Floating down the Thames in the dark was scary at first, but after a while we got used to it and found it surprisingly relaxing.

The experienced bargees on each barge manned some of the barge's oars and several stood ready at its front with very long wooden poles in their hands to push us away from trouble. They seemed to know where they were even in the darkness. I felt the bargee's obvious experience and competence very comforting and I somehow knew, despite not being able to see them in the darkness, that my men felt the same way.

There were extra oars on the barge for the bargees to use, but Andrew's men weren't allowed to touch them. As a result, they had nothing to do and everything was quiet for two or three hours except for the periodic snores and snorts of our sleepers. Several times we saw small campfires along the shore and once the delicious smell of burning meat reached out to us.

Suddenly, by the light of the partial moon, I realized there was a huge dark shape looming out of the darkness about a hundred feet ahead of us. It jolted the thinking behind my eyes and I couldn't help myself; I gave a little gasp. A few moments later there was a gentle scraping sound and a soft thud as we drifted up against one of the stone arches that were holding up the big new London bridge. The barge rocked slightly and I heard a distinct grunt as one of the bargees used his pole to push us away from the brick and rock face of the arch and we passed under the bridge.

Someone on the bridge above us must have heard the bump for a challenge was called out in French, and then again in London English. It didn't matter; one of the bargees told bridge tender he was lucky to be sitting on his arse while real men worked the river. He said it with a bit of hostility in his voice and there was no response from the bridge except for a muttered curse.

I was surprised at the exchange, and then again when the barge captain standing next to me explained that not only was such an insult normal, it was expected. In a low voice the barge captain explained that there was more than a little hostility between the bargees and the bridge tenders because the opening of the bridge "had taken coins out of the purses of many a good waterman who use to row people across the river."

If the watchman on the bridge had been able to see the barge in the moonlight, which he probably couldn't because of the clouds constantly passing in front of the moon, he would not have been alarmed; everything would have appeared quite normal—for all he would have seen were three bargees and me standing with poles in our hands and four more bargees at the oars; the archers were lying flat and unmoving on bottom of the barge under their rain skins so as to appear to be just one more of the many hundreds of cargos that moved up and down the Thames every day.

******

We reached the lower end of the Thames Pool on a partially cloudy day about two hours after the sun came up and began passing over us. It had taken us longer than expected because the river became crowded and difficult to navigate as soon as we passed the bridge and daylight arrived.

It had been both a stressful and restful passage, but in the end it was worth it—we found three of the company's galleys lashed together and anchored against the rivers flow and a fourth in the process of rowing in to join them.

My arrival in person surprised the three captains but they soon recovered. Peter was not with them and neither was Harold who accompanied them as the commander of all of the company's cogs and galleys. However, they and the galleys carrying the rest of Peter's army had sailed at the same time and were expected to be along shortly since they'd all been held back by the same unfriendly winds and weather in the Channel.

Chapter Sixteen

The encounter.

Richard and I had ridden out of Rougemont accompanied by ten horse archers. Now, as a result of sending two of the archers back to Rougemont as escorts for the girl and her two children, we were ten. Each of us was leading a good ambler remount because we wanted to make a particularly fast passage.

Normally each horse archer leads a supply horse loaded down with a bladed pike, sharpened stakes, a bale of arrows, and various other weapons and supplies. That's so he has the ability to get to the scene of a battle quickly and then dismount and fight as on foot as a weapons-heavy foot archer.

Not this time; we wanted to make the fastest passage possible in order to re-join my father and the army of archers assembling at Windsor. Accordingly, the archers' supply horses had been swapped for the riding horses of some of the archers who would be remaining at Rougemont. As a result, each of the ten of us was leading a saddled remount that was carrying only a couple of quivers of additional arrows along with two sacks of food and corn, one for the horse and one for its rider.

We were traveling with our remounts lightly loaded so each archer could keep one of his horses as fresh as possible, preferably the better and stronger of the two. It was always the prudent thing to do when one is trying to make a fast passage as couriers and outriders frequently do; one never knows when a fresh horse might be needed with no time to switch saddles and quivers.

On other hand, and there's no question about it, leading a second saddled horse can slow down a rider—until he needs a remount because the horse he is riding is unable to continue or is too tired to escape pursuers or to catch someone the rider is pursuing. Taking care of your horses and having another horse saddled and instantly available is always desirable.

****** *George*

Our first three and a half days on the London road involved almost continuous night and day riding. The only exception was when we stopped to help the girl and her children. Other than that, we had not encountered any problems and we didn't have to leave any of our horses behind, although one seemed to be developing a sore hoof and going lame. We had already distributed what was left of its cargo among the other horses. We knew that if its hoof got any worse, we'd have to drop the horse off at a smithy at one of the many villages along the road and send someone to pick it up later.

Our encounter with the young widow and her children had cost us the two men I detached to accompany them back to Rougemont. Accordingly, there were only ten of us three days later as we wearily dismounted and let our hungry and thirsty horses eat from their corn sacks and drink from the three hollowed out logs that served as watering troughs in front of the alehouse in a small and nameless farming village next to the London road.

Travelers on the road were the alehouse's main source of custom; the village itself was only about twenty daub and wattle hovels with thatched roofs, about ten of them on each side of the heavily rutted dirt cart path that came up from the road. Smoke was rising through the thatch on one of the hovels and a young boy with a switch was herding a small flock of geese with nobbled wings. Scraggly reddish chickens were scratching the ground and pecking at each other. A naked child with a thumb in her mouth stood in one of the narrow entrances staring at us.

It was a typical poor roadside village. Not one of the hovels had a chimney. Nor, for that matter, did the alehouse.

The only unique thing about the village was the very small stream that ran through the village next to the cart path running between its hovels. The flow had probably been diverted in years past so the villagers could throw their shite in the water to be carried away. We could see its residents working in the fields around it. It was an altogether peaceful scene.

We reached the village and decided to stop for a few hours after more than three days of being almost constantly in the saddle except when the horses needed a few hours of rest while they got watered and ate some of the corn from the small sacks of horse feed each of horses carried. There was no reason we stopped at that particular village except, of course, that we were exhausted and our horses needed a rest—and we could see that it had an alehouse where we might be able to get something to eat and drink.

The ale wife greeted our entrance with a big smile to show us her snaggly teeth and was soon busy dipping bowls into her barrel and setting them out in front of us on one of the wooden table that stood on the alehouse's dirt floor. There was a cooking fire in the fireplace and the low-ceiling room was smoky from the smoke that had not yet risen through the thatch.

A couple of men, traveling merchants from the look of them and the horse cart tied up outside, had glanced up in curiosity as we entered but quickly resumed their low and heated discussion when they saw we meant them no trouble. We were what we appeared to be—a band of tired and thirsty travellers taking a break from a long day on the road. If the past was any guide, we'd soon be exchanging pleasantries about the weather and asking each other about the road conditions ahead.

It was not to be. One of the horse archers who'd been outside taking care of his horses suddenly swept aside the hanging leather curtain that covered the low and narrow alehouse entrance to keep out the wind and rain, ducked his head into the smoky room, and shouted out the alarming news.

"Riders coming. Lots of them; and they're armed," he shouted as he turned around to go back outside.

"Outside, Lads. Hurry. Mount up. Time to go," I shouted as I dropped a coin on the table and headed for the opening and my horses. I was near the entrance and managed to be the second man out of the alehouse. Behind me I heard a crash as the wooden bench along the table went over. I saw one of my men take a last great gulp of ale before he ran for the door. Truth be told, so did I.

The alewife with her straggly, grey hair never said a word; she just stood there at one of her ale barrels with a look of disbelief on her face, one hand covering her open mouth and the other holding an empty bowl.

What I saw and heard when I got outside was alarming. A large body of riders and walking men was turning off the main road and coming towards us down the path to the alehouse—and there was a banner flying from a lance held by one of the horsemen.

The first of the riders pulled up in front of the alehouse as I unwrapped the reins of my two horses from the wooden hitching pole in front of the alehouse and swung myself into the saddle of my riding horse. All around me my men were rushing to do the same. It was almost certainly a baron and his knights and village levies.

Damn, I should have had a man watching the road.

"You there," a big and heavily bearded knight called as he trotted up and pulled his horse to a stop not five paces from one of my men.

"Who are you?" he demanded to know. He had the reddest beard I'd ever seen and he spoke with authority. He was probably either the baron himself or one of his more important knights.

"We're some of the Earl of Devon's men, Sir Knight," I called over to him as I waited for my men to finish mounting, and more and more of the new arrivals pulled up their horses in front of us and eyed us with suspicion.

"We're on our way to Staines to join our lord and his friends," I said as watched the last of my men finish swing himself aboard his horse. I gently kicked my horse in the ribs and pulled my reins to ride it between a couple of the riders facing me and through the group of horsemen gathering behind them.

"No. Stop them. They're not Devon's men; they're archers," someone suddenly shouted from behind the red-bearded knight.

"We're Devon's men and friendly," I desperately shouted the lie as I suddenly kicked and whipped my horse so that it lunged forward and I began trying to force my way through the gathering crowd while holding my remount's reins in my left hand so it was following close alongside. I could see my men trying to break out with me as I attempted to ride through the mob of riders—who were by then two and three deep in a semi-circle around us and beginning to draw their swords.

One brave soul among the baron's men was able to reach out and grab my remount horse by its halter as we came past him, and nearly had his arm pulled off for his trouble as my now excited horses dug in their heels and careened their way through the gathering throng of riders. Just as I cleared them I had to lean off my saddle to my left towards my remount to avoid a wild sword swing.

Once I got clear of the now-shouting and cursing horsemen, I had to haul my reins hard to the left to turn my galloping horses off the narrow village path in order avoid the men coming on foot behind the riders, some of whom were now running to join the fray.

I jumped my two horses over the little steam that had been channelled to run its waters through the village to carry away the village's shite and garbage, galloped across the field next to the village path, and re-joined the main road about five hundred paces down the road from the village path—and in the process rode right past a handful of women who had been forking hay up into a wain under the supervision of a little old man when we arrived.

Either he was very small or they were very large, for every one of the women seemed to be at least twice the size of the man. At the moment, the women were leaning on the wooden handles of their forks watching the great flurry of activity and hard riding men with impassive faces.

A number of my men had broken free and were galloping in the same general direction as me, but I couldn't immediately see how many. What I did see is that some of my men had lost their remounts and that the baron's riders were turning to ride after us in hot pursuit. And I had two problems I was sure my men shared—the bow I was carrying over my shoulder was not strung and I was riding a tired horse.

And what I remember as the most striking thing of all—as I jumped the horse over the little stream, I looked down and saw the shadows of big fish in it. There was no doubt about it, there were fish in that narrow little trickle of water and some of them were quite large.

****** *George*

Seven of us reached the London road and began riding down it towards London with what appeared to be thirty or forty riders in hot pursuit. I'd lost three men. I could see Richard riding behind me with three of the horse archers; two other archers had somehow gotten ahead of me. Richard had dropped the reins of his remount and left it behind. Two of the archers had done the same; better alive with one horse than dead with two.

Our pursuers' horses must have been real dogs for they couldn't catch us. The people travelling on the road stopped and watched in surprise as we thundered past them with our pursuers strung out and following close behind.

One after another the seven of us soon settled into the fast ambling pace that our horses could continue for hours when they were fresh, except, of course, ours were not. After what seemed like hours but was probably only twenty or thirty minutes, one after another of our pursuers began pulling up their horses and turning back. When I was far enough ahead of our remaining pursuers, I pulled my horse to a brief halt, leaned over to press the tip of my longbow against the muddy road to bend it, and strung my bow. Then I rode on.

A few minutes later, when I saw that I would have enough time, I leapt off my tired horse and jumped on to my much fresher and stronger remount. My men must have been watching because one after another they pulled up their horses and did the same, including one young archer who almost didn't get away fast enough from what was left of our pursuers because his excited remount kept shying away as he tried to climb aboard.

"Almost time for a wounded bird?" I gasped over to Richard who had closed up with me and was riding alongside of me. I didn't wait for his answer.

"Hoy Lads," I shouted as loud as I could in a voice that was somewhat out of breath from all the excitement and the many minutes of hard riding. "Get ready. We'll be doing a wounded bird as soon as the last of them quit chasing us and turn back."

****** *George*

A few minutes later, our final three pursuers pulled up their horses, turned them around, and started leisurely riding back to the village to re-join their mates. I immediately pulled my horse's head around and started after them, slowly at first so my men could form up on me, and then faster and faster.

Some of the poor sods who had finally given up trying to catch us didn't realize what was happening. They actually pulled up their horses and waited for us when they saw us ambling down the road towards them. They waited for us until it dawned on them that we weren't friendly. By then it was too late; they were well within range of our longbows when they turned their horses around and tried to escape. Not that we immediately started pushing arrows at them. To the contrary, we chased them until we got so close we couldn't miss.

I got the first one. We were riding almost side by side when I pushed an arrow deep into the side of his horse. It took five or six more steps before its front legs buckled and it somersaulted forward into the ditch running alongside the road. I looked back in time to see the archer about three horse lengths behind me lean down from his saddle and push an arrow straight into the fallen rider from just a few feet away. It was doubtful he would have gotten up from such a fall; but he certainly won't now, and probably never.

We followed our one-time pursuers down the London road back towards the little village and killed them off one after another: sometimes with an arrow into the rider; sometimes with an arrow into his horse. And the travellers who had stopped and their jaws had dropped over when we and our pursuers had thundered past on our way towards London now stopped and watched as we came back in the other direction. Almost every time one of our former pursuers saw us riding down the road towards them, he thought we were his friends who had continued to pursue us after he too had stopped and turned around, and that we too were now coming back down the road after giving up the pursuit. Several of the fools actually pulled up their horses and waited for us to reach them. It was a fatal mistake.

The only ones who got escaped us were three or four riders who were smart enough to realize what was happening and gallop off the road to one side or the other to escape. We didn't chase after them if they got far enough off the road before we reached them; we continued on past to get the horsemen who were still riding back to the village on the road ahead of us.

By the time we reached the village our horses were on their last legs and we'd left a trail of dead and wounded pursuers and their horses behind us. As far as I could tell only two or three of our pursuers had been able to outrun us and reach the village where it had all started. They were probably the smartest of them all, or, at least temporarily, the luckiest—their horses had been strong enough to catch up with us, but they had held back in order to avoid having to actually fight us.

****** *George*

We little band of seven had somehow become six by the time we pulled up our exhausted horses and began walking them back into the village. The horse of one of our number, an older one-stripe archer from York named Sam, had totally broken down on the road and collapsed several miles back. Sam rolled clear and motioned for us to keep going and began running behind us with his longbow in one hand and a quiver of arrows in the other.

At least one of our pursuers must have made it back to the little village, for when we cautiously walked our horses into the village we found the a couple of exhausted horses tied to the hitching post in front of the alehouse, and a large number of men on foot clustered together behind what must have been their version of a defensive shield wall.

My men spread out at my command so that we were in a line with about twenty paces between each of us as we began slowly walking our horses towards the shield wall until we got within hailing distance. Those of us who had escaped with our remounts had long ago mounted our best horse and left the other horse behind; we had both hands free and were ready to fight.

"We've come for our three missing men," I shouted when I got close enough to be heard. "Where are they? Bring them to us immediately and we will let you leave and go home; don't bring them and you will die. Those are your choices. What say you?"

"We're Lord Spencer's men from Northampton. We can't do anything without his lordship's permission," someone finally shouted. By then we had ridden even closer and they were easily within the range of our longbows. I raised my hand to stop my men from riding any closer. I didn't come any closer because it would bring us in range of a short bow if any of them had one or, God forbid, a crossbow.

"If Lord Spencer was one of the riders who pursued us, he's almost certainly dead or he's run for home and deserted you," I shouted. "It doesn't matter; you must produce my men immediately or we will begin killing you."

I waited and there was no answer. So be it.

"Two quick shafts on my command; heavies to go through their shields," I said first to the two riders on my right and then to the three on my left as I raised my hand with an arrow in it. My men on either side of me nocked their first arrows.

"Push two," I shouted as I dropped my hand and nocked the arrow. Our arrows went right though the shield wall and into several of the men behind it. There were great screams and shouts as they were hit.

"Once again," I shouted over to the shield wall as I stood on my stirrups and leaned forward to point my finger at them. "Your choices are to deliver our three men or to die here and now." Then I turned and delivered my orders to the riders on my left and then to those on the right.

"Four this time." I waited a few seconds and then raised my hand. This time there were many calls and shouts from the men we were facing and several of them dropped their shields and began to run away.

"We can't," someone finally shouted out to us. Sir Ridley had them killed." *My God; they've murdered my men.*

It was too much. A great black anger arose behind my eyes and overcame me. I went beserk as if I was one of the old Norman pagans Uncle Thomas had learnt us so much about. I dropped my hand and shouted "Push and don't stop; kill all the murdering bastards." That's when the screaming and killing really started.

****** *George*

The madness behind my eyes didn't last all that long. It ended when I suddenly realized that the Northampton men were throwing down their arms and trying to surrender. And when the last arrow had been pushed and it was all over, we didn't kill them. Killing enemy wounded and prisoners was not something archers were allowed to do except with pirates; they get tossed into the sea no matter what their condition.

Of course, we were learnt to always accept surrenders; if an enemy thinks he'll be killed if he surrenders, he'll just keep fighting and some of our own men may be killed or wounded unnecessarily. That's what Uncle Thomas always told us and he was right.

After the Northampton survivors had thrown down their arms and we'd stopped pushing out arrows, we helped the unwounded Northampton men pull their wounded friends and neighbours into the shade provided by one of the village hovels. There was water nearby and they would no doubt be helped after we left by the villagers and their returning friends—those who escaped by running out into the surrounding fields or were still standing when we finally stopped pushing out arrows.

My blind anger was long gone from behind my eyes by the time a totally exhausted Sam, still carrying his longbow and a quiver of arrows, staggered into the village while we were picking up weapons and giving mercies to the Northampton men who needed them.

Sam nodded back and smiled gratefully when I acknowledged his effort with a smile and waved him over to the alehouse while mouthing a wordless suggestion to him that he have a bowl. The alewife standing in its entry saw the exchange. She nodded and smiled her toothless agreement as she held aside the hanging door skin and motioned for Sam to enter.

To the great delight of me and my men, one of the wounded men we captured was Sir Ridley, the Spencer knight who had ordered the murder of our three fellow archers. He'd taken an arrow in the hip and couldn't run.

"You look like a pirate to me," I said as I chopped his neck with a captured axe. Then I staggered over to the alehouse to join Sam for a bowl of ale and put my head down on the table for a sleep.

Chapter Seventeen

A surprise visitor

One after another the three narrow river barges moored themselves to our galleys and began unloading the archers they had carried down the river during the night. Then we settled down to wait for Peter and the rest of his army to arrive.

It was a cheerful time and archers of Andrew Small's company were soon exchanging stories with their friends among the archers who had just arrived from on the galleys from Cornwall, eating pieces of cheese and newly cooked flatbreads and meat strips, and participating in the inevitable archery and moors dancing contests.

The bargees were content to remain with us. They sat in the sun dicing and drinking from a wineskin that had appeared as if by magic and watched the archery and moors dancing. We had paid to wait with us because we didn't want them moving back up the Thames and telling the barons' men that Peter's army had arrived and how many archers had been put ashore. It was probably a meaningless thing to do, paying them that is, because you didn't need to be an alchemist to count the number of arriving galleys, estimate the number of archers on each of them, and know the size of the army of archers arriving from Cornwall to reinforce the King John.

Almost immediately, I had myself rowed the short distance to the riverbank in one of the galleys dinghies. As soon as I got ashore I employed one of the local lads with a horse cart to ride into London with a message for Old Freddy at the stables next to the quay where the company's galleys usually moor—bring at least ten wains, and preferably as many as twenty, down the road running alongside the Thames as soon as possible. We'll need them for a week or so to help carry our equipment and supplies to Windsor.

I briefly thought about giving my messenger a few more coins and having him bring back a jar of juniper brew from the White Horse, but I didn't.

The archers of course could carry everything themselves. But, if they did, everyone including the French knights and the rebellious barons, would immediately know about one of the new weapons we didn't want the barons and their French allies to see, at least not until they were too close to avoid being chopped by them—our hooked and bladed pikes attached to long wooden poles. The wains could also carry the sharpened stakes that the archers use to discourage mounted attacks and the archers' leather tents.

****** *William*

Our galleys and the barges stayed anchored together just off the riverbank all the rest of that day and most of the next morning, until all of Harold's galleys carrying Peter's army had arrived. The waiting time was well spent. Those of Peter's men who had already arrived ate like horses and quickly recovered from their storm-tossed journey down the Channel; less than an hour after each galley's arrival, moors dancing and archery practice inevitably covered every inch of its deck space. The men's morale was sky high.

As soon as Harold, Peter, and I saw the last galley coming up the river, our already-arrived galleys were ordered to move to the riverbank and begin unloading their archers and equipment. The wains had arrived hours earlier and were waiting. There were twenty two wains; Freddy himself had ridden with them and brought a couple of spares in case a horse or wheel broke down.

It took a couple of hours to bring all the archers and their weapons and supplies ashore. By the time we were finished we had attracted quite a growing crowd of onlookers, everything from street girls and their protectors to small merchants selling bowls of wine from a wineskins slung over their shoulders and large merchants offering to supply each galley with everything it might need for a long voyage. It got so chaotic that Peter ended up placing a line of guards to keep everyone away. That's when we brought the bladed pikes ashore, wrapped in rain skins so they couldn't be seen, and loaded them in the wains.

Freddy had gone back to London and I was standing with Peter and Harold watching the last of the archers carry their equipment ashore when a tall and gangly, tonsured and bearded priest, wearing his hood up so he would be hard to recognize unless he was looking straight at you, hurried towards me and Peter with a big smile on his face. For a brief moment I didn't recognize him, but then I did and my eyes widened with surprise and pleasure. It was Alfred.

Father Alfredo, as he is currently and perhaps temporarily named, had been just plain Alfred when we first met years ago on Cyprus when he was an orphan boy and the same age as George. He was one of Thomas's very first students and one of George's oldest and dearest friends. It was if I'd known him forever as a son.

Alfred had been Thomas's best student at gobbling Latin and more interested in books and alchemy than in becoming an archer. As a result, and at Thomas's insistence, we'd made a position for him elsewhere, as one of our priestly spies. As a result, Alfred is currently in the household of the Pope's nuncio to King John—a prestigious appointment resulting from a substantial pouch of coins he had carried from Rome a couple of years ago along with a letter from a recently deceased close friend of the nuncio asking him to look after his son "Alfredo." As you might well imagine, the nuncio welcomed the young priest and the coins into his household with open arms.

I didn't want to destroy Alfred's cover in case anyone was watching. Accordingly, it was with the greatest difficulty that I resisted giving the lad a great and manly hug; I couldn't do that, of course, for it would have drawn attention to him and possibly endangered him. Instead, in a low and somewhat emotional voice so that only Peter and

Harold could overhear, I told Alfred most sincerely that I was pleased to see him looking so healthy and that he should consider himself as having been ferociously hugged and most warmly welcomed. He smiled gratefully and nodded his understanding.

George and Thomas think he's a fine fellow and very brave and loyal, and that's all I need to know.

What we learned from Alfred was important, including why he had come to us instead of sending a message to Thomas. Until recently, Alfred explained in a low voice for fear of being overheard, he had been in Windsor assisting the nuncio at the king's court and able to periodically slip away at night to give information to Thomas when Thomas came to Windsor to report to the king on the status of the peace conference. He was now, however, in London and unable to safely communicate with Thomas because the nuncio had recently moved to London and, of course, taken Alfred and the rest of his household with him.

It soon became clear as we talked that Alfred had taken a great risk by slipping away to meet us. He'd only done so because he'd recently learned new and vital information—for one, the latest message from the Pope ordered Cardinal Langton to continue holding peace talks between the barons and King John, but did *not* threaten the barons with excommunication or any other penalties for opposing the king.

According to what Alfred heard yesterday when standing silently behind the nuncio when the nuncio met with the commander of the French knights, the barons and French were ecstatic and encouraged by the Holy Father's inaction and confident that the king and his supporters would be distraught and discouraged. Their priests supporting the French and the barons agreed and constantly assured them that they were doing "God's will."

Alfred had brought the information to us because his ability to take it to Thomas had ended several weeks ago. That's when the Nuncio lied to the king and said he'd received a message from Rome ordering him to leave the court and go to London and work on getting French out of London. In fact, according to Alfred, the nuncio moved back to London, not to encourage the French to leave as he had told King John and his courtiers when he explained his departure, but to welcome and assist Louis, the crown prince and heir to the throne of France—to whom the barons had offered the throne of England in exchange for French help in getting rid of King John.

"There is no question about it," Father Alfred told Peter and me in a low voice as we leaned our heads together. "The nuncio thinks the Holy Father's lack of support for King John means French crown prince will soon be England's king and, thus, the man with whom he should be close."

Alfred had come to warn us about more than that the French and barons were greatly encouraged by the Holy Father's inaction; they had, he told us, heard last night that an army of archers would be landing south of London and marching to Windsor to support the king. That we were now here in the London area and would be marching to Windsor to support King John was not much of a secret.

What he told us next, however, explained why he'd taken the risk of coming, and greatly surprised me and caused black thoughts behind my eyes—the commander of the French knights in London, a certain Jean du Bureau, had decided to attack and destroy Peter's army before it could link up with the king's forces at Windsor. They were also expecting French reinforcements to arrive momentarily.

According to Alfred, du Bureau had spent the morning calling in his forces from London's various fortresses. They were assembling in a cemetery near the bridge and were waiting to see if we would march through the city to get to Windsor or march up the road that ran along the Thames.

The French plan, if we marched through the city, was to attack us from both ends of a long and narrow lane from which there was no outlet; if we marched up the road that ran along the Thames, we would be attacked where the road curved around the entrance to the new bridge. It made sense.

Alfred, in turn, was greatly surprised to hear the size and extent of our victory over Devon's army and the ease with which we turned back FitzWalter's attack. The French, he was sure, did not know about the destruction of Devon's army or the extent of FitzWalter's defeat.

"We'd heard rumours of the recent fighting near Windsor involving some archers, of course, but everyone in London thinks they were only exaggerations related to the minor skirmishes that are occurring more and more frequently these days between the king's supporters and the barons and French. They just cannot believe an army led by veteran knights can be defeated by commoners from Cornwall.

"And Cyprus, of course," he added mischievously with a twinkle in his eye."

****** *William*

"Alfred's right," Peter said as Alfred hurried away with his face looking at the ground so he couldn't be recognized. "They'll be on foot and try to pen us up in a narrow street if we go through the city or they'll be waiting for us where the road along the river narrows at the new bridge if we try to march up the Thames."

We talked about it and I tried to remember the details of an old map of the city of London Thomas had shown me years ago. I couldn't.

After much discussion, we decided to wait and leave tonight after it gets dark–and walk all the way around the city instead of through it or along the Thames. If the French knights wanted to fight, they'd have to come out of the city to do it.

Then I had another idea.

******

Alfred was hardly out of sight when we had yet another visitor, a friend Peter and I also hadn't seen for several years. Indeed, I had watched David Levi and one of his sons arrive in a horse cart out of the corner of my eye while the three of us were talking to Alfred. They had deliberately hung back in order to avoid having to meet the unknown priest with whom we were huddled and speaking most private.

What was interesting and immediately caught my attention was that they were dressed to fit into the crowd of bargees and merchants on the quay, and so too was their ragged cart driver and the four "workmen" in the second horse cart that had arrived close behind them. All five of them were almost certainly heavily armed; I got that impression because I was almost positive that everyone including David was wearing a chain shirt under his rough and dirty workman's gown.

David and his son, I think I recalled his name as Issak, waited until Alfred was out of sight before they approached with their men fanning out behind them in a protective circle. We greeted each other with the broad smiles, handshakes, and the hugs and exclamations of old friends and good customers who had been reunited after a long absence. And, of course, we began by exchanging the traditional pleasantries and inquiries about our families and our children and wives.

Peter, Harold, and I greeted the two Levis as the true friends they had many times over proved themselves to be. Even so, it was good that David and his son had not approached us when we were talking to Albert; David and his fellow Jewish merchants were another reliable source of information and custom, one that Albert didn't need to know about just as the Levis didn't need to know about Albert being one of us, or even that he knew us.

"News travels fast these days; all of London knows you are here from Cornwall with your archers and everyone wonders what it means?" said a beaming David Levi, the king's principal money lender and one of London's leading merchants.

"We'd heard you had come to London with two armies of archers for King John so I came to see for myself and, hopefully, have a chance to talk with you. Issak came with me in hopes of seeing George. Is he well?" David inquired; he said not a word about the guards he'd brought with him.

It took some time and conversation, but it became clear that David was seeking both information and advice—he wanted to know what I thought was going to happen to the king and whether he should continue to help King John financially. "Frankly, we're worried that the king already owes us so much money that he'll turn on us to avoid repaying it.

"It's not the priests and the church we're worried about," David said with a sigh as he continued. "It's the king. He owes us too much money and wants to borrow more."

"Well, he should be able to pay," I said. "He's likely to hold on to the crown, although one can never be sure about such things."

"That's not it. I agree with you, William. I think John will hold on and win in the end over the barons and the French. But then what will he do? He owes us so much I'm worried that he will slaughter the Jews to avoid paying us."

"I'd be worried if I were you," I sombrely agreed as his son listened intently. "So I'd keep a fast galley close at hand and come to me in Cornwall or Cyprus if there is any trouble. Good friends and their families and friends are always welcome and you are a good friend."

****** *William*

Traffic on the Thames had been heavy going in both directions while we were unloading the archers and talking to Alfred and the Levis, and there were fishermen all along the riverbanks on both sides and even a few fishing from little dinghies tied to the riverbank. Unfortunately, and to our great dismay, the inbound boats and barges coming up the river included a great bulky French horse transport and two French cogs loaded with French knights and their squires and servants.

It was the French reinforcements and they were arriving in time to be used against us.

We watched and were watched in turn as the two cogs and the horse transport were towed slowly past us by unfamiliar war galleys and berthed just up the river opposite the livestock market. According to David Levi's son, the quay near the livestock market was as far up the river as a livestock carrier could go and still reach a quay that was high enough above the water such that the horses, cattle, and sheep on its deck could walk off their transport. If the horse transport went any further upstream the horses would have to be lifted off one at a time in slings.

There was no mistaking what each of us saw as the French came gliding slowly past us and their way upstream—they saw an army of English archers and we saw an army of French knights.

The French began mooring their boats and Peter and I sent our apprentices walking up the road along the riverbank to watch them and count. David and his son had barely slipped away when I noticed a very small party of men, only three, break away from the hectic unloading activity of the French knights and begin walking towards us.

Peter and I were with Harold aboard a galley moored to the riverbank when we saw them coming. We each grabbed a short sword and a small galley shield, vaulted over the railing, and began to walk up the road along the river to meet them, leaving our longbows behind.

Of course, we went out to meet them; we were curious. And besides, we didn't want them to get close enough to see that the bows over almost every man's shoulder was a longbow and that we had large numbers of bladed pikes in our wains in addition to the two sharpened stakes each archer is responsible for bringing to a battle.

We eyed each other with wary curiosity as the distance between us closed. Approaching us were a tall and stately monk, a burly French knight with white hair, and man dressed as the sailing master of a cog might dress. What was abundantly clear was that it was the monk who was the leader of the three; and what was a surprise was that the monk greeted us in Norman-accented English and I immediately knew who he was even though we'd never met.

"Hello William of Cornwall," the monk said as he held out his hand with an engaging smile. "We've never met but I recognize you from the number of stripes on your tunic. I am Eustace Buskett, admiral of the French channel fleet. They called me Eustace the Monk when I was the admiral of King John's channel fleet."

"Yes, I've heard of you, Monsieur Buskett," I said as I took his hand. "You are a famous man. What brings you to England?"

Of course I've heard of you; you're the pirate based in the channel islands who is famous for betraying his English men when he changed sides. Why did you change sides and go from supporting King John and preying on French shipping to opposing King John and preying on English shipping?

"Why, I'm here for the money, of course. I'm a mercenary just like you and your archers. And the French have more coins than King John."

We introduced our companions, commented on the weather that we'd recently encountered in the Channel and the difficulty of unloading horses, agreed that it was a good thing that we hadn't tried to take any of each other's cogs and galleys, and assured each other of our hope that we would meet again under more pleasant circumstances.

I told Eustace and his friend the same lies our men had been told—that we would be camping here by the side of the Thames until our final two galleys arrived. Our meeting was brief and our parting was amiable; they didn't see or count our weapons. *Of course I lied about waiting for two more galleys to arrive; I didn't want them to know we would be moving soon,*

"Are you thinking what I'm thinking?" I asked Peter and Harold as we walked back to our men.

Chapter Eighteen

News from home.

George woke up with a snort when one of his men sat down next to him at the alehouse table on which he had been resting his head. He must have been asleep for several hours for it was already late in the afternoon. To his surprise, while he was sleeping he had somehow decided that taking the armour and weapons he and his men had collected from Spencer's men to Windsor was important even if it meant getting there a day later than he had originally planned.

At least that's what he woke up knowing he would do—keep them. There was also the not so unimportant reality that the armour and weapons were valuable and would yield prize coins for him and his men when they were sold.

****** *George*

My men and I spent what was left of the day burying our three murdered men and sending off our almost one hundred prisoners to begin walking home without their weapons. Before they were allowed to leave, however, I had them collect Lord Spencer's dead, at least those whose bodies were in the village, and stack them up in the field next to the village. To their credit, some of the released prisoners stayed and buried their dead.

After I awoke from my nap, I'd left Richard in command of our prisoners and gone out with a wain from the village and a couple of archers to strip the dead and wounded riders on the road of their valuables. We were too late: travellers and the local villagers had already stripped them and carried away their weapons and saddles and butchered their horses.

The wounded riders had either died or disappeared. The only exception was one poor soul we found hiding in some trees. He was sweating and trembling with a broken leg and an arrow through his arm. He and the wounded in the village were carried into an empty hovel to be barbered by their friends.

Lord Spencer and his knights and their squires had not been wearing their armour when they first arrived in the village, and they had not taken the time to don it before galloping off to chase after us. They had not expected to meet us any more than we had expected to meet them. As a result, they had been carrying their armour along with their tents and food supplies in a couple of wains which they left behind when they went off chasing after us—and now we had their wains full of armour and all the captured weapons as well.

Our taking of the two wains full of armour and capturing the weapons of Lord Spencer and his men changed everything. They were valuable and none of us wanted to risk losing the prize money the armour and weapons would fetch when they were sold. Accordingly, and to my men's great relief, I announced a change in the route we would follow on our trip to Windsor. Now we would now travel to Windsor via the ford at Oxford instead of riding directly and swimming our horses across the river.

The only alternative would be to follow the old Roman road all the way to London, cross the Thames on the new bridge, and ride north to Windsor. That's a route which we didn't dare to travel because the barons and the French were reported to be holding London.

Taking a roundabout route through Oxford would add at least one additional day to our travels and perhaps two depending on the road, but it would let us walk our horses and wains across the Thames where the road went through the ford used by the ox carts instead of trying to swim the horses and wains across the Thames near Windsor where the river is much deeper.

Of course, I changed our route; it wouldn't do to lose our prize money by having the wains sink or overturn and dump the armour and the weapons into the river where the water was so deep we'd never recover them.

Late that evening I fell asleep on the floor of the alehouse wondering what my share of the prize money would be and why the men of Spencer's levies hadn't all suddenly run in every direction at the same time or immediately thrown down their arms and surrendered when we began attacking them. A few of them did and got away, but most did not. If they had run, almost all of them would have escaped.

But they didn't run. Why? It was the last thing I remembered.

****** *George*

We ate fresh bread and what was left of some chickens the alewife had burned for us to eat the previous day, drank a couple of bowls of morning ale to refresh ourselves, and left the little village a few minutes after the sun arrived.

Seven of us rode out of the village; five riding on our now-rested and restored amblers and two driving the wains we had taken off the Northampton men. The wains were fully loaded with the captured swords and other weapons piled on top of the captured armour. The horses of the archers driving the wains were tied to the rear of the wains and plodded dutifully along behind them.

It was a quiet departure. The village's farmers had already walked out to their fields and no one was there to wave us off and bid farewell as we clattered out of the village towards the still-empty London Road. It was as if yesterday's death and destruction had never happened. Yesterday was to the village like a rock dropped into a pond whose ripples had long ago disappeared.

Three days later we splashed our way across the Thames, clattered down the cobblestoned main street of Oxford, and pulled up outside the great wooden gate of St.

Frideswide Priory where Uncle Thomas and the other members of the king's peace council were meeting. One of the gatekeepers ran to get him. He came immediately.

"George? Is it really you? I could hardly believe it when the gatekeeper came in and told me you were here. Oh Welcome, Welcome indeed lad," he said as he gave me a big hug. "It's good to see you, and you too, Richard. *Who also got a hug.* But why are you here?"

Uncle Thomas was astonished and got increasingly excited as we stood in the main entrance to the priory and told him about our battle with Lord Spencer and his Northampton men, and showed him the armour and weapons we had collected from the battlefield.

"Seven of you? Just seven did for them one at a time until they surrendered? The king will be overbalanced with joy when he hears. We must go to Windsor immediately to tell him. There's not a moment to spare. It's just the thing to raise his spirits and light a fire under his supporters." *And discourage the barons and French from attacking the king so that we suffer more casualties.*

We drove the wains through the gate and into priory's courtyard for safe-keeping, and the nine of us repaired to the nearby Horse and Bull Alehouse for some food and something to drink, the ninth being Uncle Thomas's new apprentice sergeant, a lad from our school by the name of Nolan whose father was a smith in a village outside of Chester belonging to the Earl of Chester. Nolan Smith had been several years behind Richard and me and much better than most of us when it came to gobbling in Latin.

"I have some joyous family news for you William," said Uncle Thomas as we walked to the Horse and Bull just as a light rain began to fall. "It just came in today by courier from Cornwall.

"All of your family are well and Tori has given you a brother, who will be baptized as Robert, Robert Courtenay, when I get back to Cornwall. We'll fiddle the church records to make him a lord and you as well. You're the heir to the earldom, of course, and he's your second. Your father doesn't know about young Robert yet. He'll be pleased."

"Courtenay?" I asked. I was as pleased about the name as I expected my father would be about my new brother. I knew he had been thinking about taking a family name for us for a long time, but I somehow expected him to use Archer or Cornwall. But Courtenay? *I like it.*

"Your father finally decided he needed a family name so he chose Courtenay because of its connection to Okehampton, at least that's what he told me," said Uncle Thomas with a smile. He clearly approved of the decision.

******

We all stayed in Oxford in Uncle Thomas's tiny room at the top of the stairs that rainy night and the nine of us left for Windsor early the next morning with an additional hired wain in case one of ours broke down. According to Uncle Thomas, "If we keep moving and the road isn't washed out or too crowded we might be able make Windsor before nightfall."

Chapter Nineteen

Fighting on the river

"Everyone take your weapons out of the wains and re-board your galleys; we will be floating down the river to a safer place to camp. The wains will follow on the river road with the tents and food supplies." Peter emphasized the word *safer* as he shouted out the order. That order was followed almost immediately by "All captains report to the commander's galley."

Peter's totally unexpected orders were quickly picked up and loudly repeated by the sergeants and their chosen men. Within seconds the quiet and relaxed riverbank and our galleys were turned into beehives of activity with cursing sergeants and running men. The numerous onlookers and merchants gaped in surprise and began asking each other what it meant.

"Well," I asked Peter and Harold as we stood on the roof of the rear castle of Peter's galley and watched the frenzied activity a few feet away on the riverbank and on the nearby galleys. "This will certainly get the attention of Eustace and the French. How much do you think it will alarm them?

"They'll notice it, alright. But they'll probably think we're moving because we're afraid of them. They'll probably relax as soon as our galleys begin moving down the river and they see the wagons heading down the river road to follow them."

"That's what I think too," I said. "We can tell the captains our plans and give them their assignments when we're out of sight around the bend. We can row back up from there."

"What are you going to tell the company captains to do to get their men ready?" Harold asked with a smile as our apprentices listened intently.

"Why, that because of the danger of a French attack, you're going to hold a weapons inspection on every galley as soon as we reach our next anchorage further down the river, of course. We're afraid of the French knights aren't we?" I said as I smiled back and poked him on the shoulder.

Peter roared with laughter.

The sun was high overhead, the river was crowded with traffic, and the riverbank was packed with our archers, merchants, fishermen, and numerous onlookers. They did not know it yet, but there was going to be a sea battle on the Thames and they were going to have an up close and personal view of it.

****** *William*

The captains were all nearby and came quickly to get their new orders. We didn't tell them anything about our decision to raid the French galleys and transport that very day—for fear the word would almost certainly spread amongst the throngs of people gathered on the riverbank and the French would have time prepare for our raid.

Accordingly, the only thing our seven galley captains were told as each arrived and climbed up on to the castle roof to join us was that the French knights were too close for comfort and that he was to re-load his men and weapons immediately, rendezvous with Harold's galley downstream below the next bend in the river, and then follow us to where we would all once again tie up and unload our men.

Each of the galley captains hurried away determined not to be the last to load his men and weapons and start down the river towards the rendezvous. Andrew Small was told to spread his men among the galleys and attach himself to Harold to serve as his assistant.

"A good plan today that surprises our enemies is better than a perfect plan tomorrow that doesn't, particularly when the French will probably be finished unloading their horses and be gone before we can take their galleys and transports as prizes. It will be too late tomorrow morning and too dark tonight; so we're going to hit them now before they can get themselves organized to fight us off."

That's what I leaned over told our wide-eyed apprentices as the last of the captains rushed away to get his galley ready to move down the Thames. *Sometimes I think my scarred face scares them more than my words and my rank.*

******

It may have taken several hours for the galleys to unload all their men and stow their weapons in Freddy's wains, but it seemed to take only a few minutes for the archers to snatch up their weapons and re-board their galleys. Even Harold was impressed.

"That's the last of them," he said with smug satisfaction and a nod as he ordered his sailing sergeant to stop rowing to hold his galley in place against the flow of the river, turn the bow of his galley to point in the other direction, and head downstream to the rendezvous just beyond the next curve in the river.

It didn't take long at all for our seven galleys to row down the Thames and move far enough around the next bend in the river so the new bridge and the French fleet were no longer in sight.

"I'd be obliged, Lieutenant Commander," I said to Harold a few minutes later after we passed through the bend and a handful of his oarsmen once again began to row to hold his galley in place against the flow of the river, "if you would send a man up the mast to wave the *all captains* flag."

We'd become formal as was our tradition when actual or practice war orders were being given; our men seemed to be comforted by it.

"Aye, Commandant; a man up the mast to wave the *all captains* flag," Harold answered as he stood up straight and knuckled his head; and a moment later roared out the order. He'd had a man standing by and the flag waving began almost instantly.

The captains of the galleys, which were being rowed to maintain their position around Harold's galley, were quickly alongside of Harold's in their dinghies and climbing aboard. They and my lieutenants and our apprentices were soon seated on their arses on the deck in front of me and listening intently.

It had already begun to dawn on the captains that they weren't there to receive orders to unload their archers and prepare to march them to Windsor, probably because of the nature of the activity they saw on Harold's galley as they climbed aboard—his men were already stringing their longbows, opening their arrow bales, and laying out their grappling irons and boarding ladders.

****** *Willliam*

It didn't take long to give each of the increasingly excited galley captains his specific target from among the French fleet. We had seven galleys and there were six Frenchmen—three of Eustace's galleys plus the two cogs and the horse transport that the galleys had towed up the river. Each of our galleys was assigned to take one of them with Harold's galley held in reserve to join in wherever Harold and I thought it was needed most.

Of course the captains were excited; the scent of prize money and a chance to distinguish themselves was in the air.

Boarding and taking an enemy prize was something our men knew how to do. Our sergeants and veterans had done it multiple times, and even our newest one-stripers had been learnt what to do and been made to practice it over and over again. There were very few questions because there were very few unknowns—every man had seen the French and marked them as they had slowly come past us as they made their way upstream.

The only real question was one no one could answer—how many of the French knights and soldiers would still be on board the cogs and horse transport when we reached them, and would they and Eustace's men fight or run.

****** *Harold*

Our galleys came back up the river like a pack of wolves on a hunt when William ordered me to wave the *follow me* flag and we began moving up the Thames. We were all soon moving at top speed because we had two men pulling hard at every oar. It was a very deliberate effort to close with the French quickly before they had enough warning time to organize a resistance.

We were moving so fast that our hair and clothing were whipping in the wind and the people on the boats and barges we passed gaped as we went flying by them as if they were standing still. It was quite thrilling and there were several near-collisions. The rowing drums were going as fast and loud as I'd ever heard them.

Then the unexpected happened. Coming down the river towards us was one of Eustace's three galleys. It must have finished towing one of the French transports up the river to unload near the city walls just below the bridge and now was being sent elsewhere. Its captain obviously didn't know we were coming; it was proceeding slowly and normally down the Thames with only a few of its oars in the water for the steerage it needed to pick its way through the traffic on the river.

William and I were standing on the roof of the forward castle and first saw the French galley moving towards us as we began passing through one of the bends in the Thames where it flows around London. I'm not sure I know why, but William made an instant decision to take it.

"It's one of Eustace's, by God," he said to me as it came into sight. Then he surprised me. "Take the bastard, Harold. Pass her close and throw your grapples; stop waving the *follow me* flag" There was no hesitation or question in his voice. It was an order.

"Aye, Commandant, pass her close and throw my grapples; stop waving the *follow me* flag," I instantly responded and began shouting my orders.

We were almost on her when I saw someone on the roof of the Frenchman's front castle begin waving his arms about and rush to the edge of the roof to begin shouting orders down to his rowing deck. We'd been seen, but too late for the on-coming French galley, or so it seemed.

My sailor lads on the port side of my galley began swinging their grapples around and around their heads in great circles and Tim my rudder man turned our bow so we went straight at the oncoming Frenchie. At the same time the archers on the upper rowing bench put down their oars, picked up their longbows, and moved out on to the deck.

All the while William was waving his right arm in great circular pointing motions to our other galleys and shouting over the water to them, "Keep going ... Keep going ... Don't stop... Keep going."

We closed quickly on the French galley but not quickly enough. All of a sudden more of the Frenchman's oars began to row and it began to make a hard turn away from us and towards the distant riverbank. As a result, instead of coming directly alongside, our bow just clipped the Frenchman's stern without taking out any of its oars.

The collision caused many of us to stagger and fall down onto our knees and all of our grapples missed except the first one thrown from the very front of our galley. It hooked the very corner of the Frenchman's deck railing behind its main castle. If it hadn't hooked it, I would have had to order my galley to spin around and chase it down.

What happened next should have been expected, but it wasn't, at least not by me: The grapple line tightened as it was pulled out to its full length in the blink of an eye, and there was a great shock as it took effect. The two galleys were moving in opposite directions and both galleys were suddenly stopped dead in the water as the line tightened, and held.

Both galleys were moving when the line tightened so it did more than just stop them—it pulled the Frenchman's stern so hard that its bow stopped heading for the distant riverbank and began, instead, swinging to once again point downstream. At the same time, it pulled our bow so hard to port that almost everyone, including me, became overbalanced and fell down once again.

But the line only held temporarily. Almost immediately there was a great cracking and breaking sound as part of the Frenchman's deck railing was torn completely away with our grapple still holding it. There were shouts and screams everywhere, both from the crashes and from the arrows the archers lining our deck were pouring into the Frenchmen a few short feet away—and the two galleys began drifting apart.

"Hard to port by a quarter; all ahead full." I screamed down to Tim and my rowing sergeant. "Ready grapples." *Again.* William and his apprentice were standing next to me. I could hear their grunts as they joined the archers who had regained their feet and began pushing arrow after arrow into the men on the Frenchman's deck.

Our archers were numerous and they worked the Frenchman's deck as I gave my new sailing orders. Within the space of five or six heart beats there was no one left standing on the Frenchman's deck or castle roofs for our archers to target. The archers up above in our two nests on the mast, however, were able to see down into the Frenchman's hull and continued to push arrow after arrow into its lower rowing deck and rudder men—and, I suddenly realized, were desperately calling for more arrows as they did.

After a wobbling start, we quickly caught up with Frenchman and came alongside. It didn't take long because our entire lower rowing deck was fully manned. This time almost all of our grapples went into the Frenchman and our galley was quickly lashed to its side. Our boarding party consisted of all of the archers on our deck. They and a hastily told off prize crew of sailors instantly vaulted over the railings and onto the Frenchman's deck screaming their battle cries.

The stunned and unprepared men on the French galley never had a chance.

"We've got her ... Cast off ... cast off, I say ... and follow our galleys up the river," William ordered.

Chapter Twenty

River battle.

We cast off from the now-drifting French galley leaving almost all of our boarding party still on board her, and hurried up the river despite having none of Harold's regular oarsman, the archers now on our French prize, available to row on our upper tier of oars. As a result, orders were quickly given and every available man, including me and Harold and our apprentices, grabbed an oar and helped row until we got the galley's bow pointed up the river once again and were well and truly underway.

Until Harold and I put down our oars a couple of minutes later and hurried to the roof of the forward castle, only the sailing sergeant was on deck calling out the orders to the rowers and rudder men.

And my arms were already sore from rowing and pushing out arrows; I am surely getting too old for this.

Our galleys and the French galleys and transports they had grappled could be seen as soon as we came around the next bend in the Thames. The Frenchmen were all moored at the quay where they had been unloading their men and horses; our galleys were lashed to them and protruding further out into the stream. Boarding ladders ran up from our galley decks to the decks of the cogs and the horse transport.

As we got closer I climbed the mast and, a minute or two later, I could see a melee of fighting men on the deck of one of the French cogs, a big two-master, and that some of our men and their boarding ladders were down on the deck of our galley below it, casualties of the fighting.

The decks of all but one of the Frenchmen were crowded with men and appeared to be peaceful. We had taken the French fleet by surprise and most of the men on their decks were wearing archers' tunics. The quay, on the other hand, was covered with what were obviously fleeing French soldiers and sailors and a large crowd of astonished onlookers. The Frenchmen had obviously jumped over the deck railing of their cog to escape.

"Make for the fighting on yonder deck," I shouted down to Harold as I pointed to the French cog with one of our galleys lashed to its side. It was the only one where the fighting was still continuing.

"Aye, make for the fighting," Harold replied and promptly began shouting the necessary orders to his sailing sergeant so that both his rudder men and the rowing sergeant could hear him and prepare to get things underway even before his sailing sergeant repeated his order back to him.

Many of our most experienced fighting men and best archers were on the deck of the galley we had just taken and immediately left behind. What Harold and I now had with us on his galley were the less-experienced younger archers who had been deliberately placed on the lower tier of benches. But I had no reservations about leading them into battle—they were all fully trained and they had their experienced file sergeants and chosen men to lead them. As such, the archers who were still on board were more than a match, so far as my lieutenants and sergeants and I were concerned, for any similar-sized enemy fighting force no matter who was in it or how they were armed.

There was no doubt about it—the ability of trained Englishmen armed with the most modern of weapons to defeat a more numerous enemy was a matter of belief of all of us veterans of the company of archers fully as strong as the belief of church's faithful that properly made signs of the cross and adequate tithes and donations made prayers come true.

****** *William*

Harold and his sailing sergeant let us down. They brought our galley in too fast and didn't back its oars in time to prevent us from banging into the side of Dirk's galley with a great crash. We hit hard, way too hard, despite the efforts of Harold's sailors and some of the archers to cushion the collision by using their poles and pike handles to hold us off and cushion the blow.

Despite the hit and the damage it undoubtedly caused, Harold and I picked ourselves up and led our shouting and screaming archers over the deck railing and on to Dirk's galley even before our sailors started lashing our galley to it.

We had to cross the deck of Dirk's galley in order to reach the fighting going on above us on the deck of the French cog. Crossing the deck was easy because it was totally empty except for a dozen or so men in archers' tunics who were lying on the deck as a result of being killed or wounded.

As we boarded Dirk's galley and ran across the deck, it became instantly clear from the noise and commotion above us that the French on this cog were continuing to resist. Dirk and his able-bodied men were all above us on the deck of the French cog fighting for their lives and prize money.

It was also instantly obvious what had happened—the Frenchmen on the cog had seen Dirk's galley coming and been able to get to their cog's deck railing in time to push over some of the boarding ladders that Dirk and his men were raising in an effort to climb up to their deck. On the other hand, the French sailors and soldiers clearly hadn't pushed over all of them; Dirk and his men had managed to climb up those that had remained and were now on the French deck. There was nothing for us to do except put more boarding ladders in place and follow them up.

It all happened in a few short heartbeats. We ran across deck of Dirk's galley with our own boarding ladders and raised them while, at the same time, others of our men began raising some of Dirk's boarding ladders which had been thrown down and were lying haphazardly on his galley's deck amongst his dead and wounded.

I held a ladder for some of Harold's archers to climb and then nervously climbed it myself. What I saw when I got high enough on the ladder to see the deck of the French cog was a large number of Dirk's men grouped at the stern of the French galley facing a large of French soldiers and sailors in the bow. They weren't really fighting; they were mostly shouting and shaking their weapons at each other. What shocked me was that all of Dirk's men were carrying short swords and galley shields instead of their longbows and quivers. Someone had made a great mistake.

Our arrival quickly turned the tide. Harold's men climbed the hastily erected and re-erected boarding ladders carrying their longbows and quivers slung over their shoulders and quickly put them to work. The surviving Frenchmen just as quickly threw down their arms. Some of them surrendered; most, however, escaped by jumping down from the Frenchman's deck on to the nearby quay and disappearing into the large and rapidly growing crowd of onlookers.

There was much shouting, pointing, and running about as the arrows began flying and the fighting ended almost instantly. Two more of our galleys also arrived right behind Harold's. Their crews also came hurrying across Dirk's deck carrying their boarding ladders. The deck of the French cog was soon so packed with archers that Harold and I had to begin sending them away.

Peter was on one of the second of the new arrivals and became absolutely beside himself with rage as soon as he saw Dirk's casualties and realized what had happened. If he'd been the commander on the scene instead of me, I think he would have cut Dirk down or hung him on the spot. There will be a captains' court for sure.

It was a great victory and there would be lots of prize money, but it appeared as though we'd lost men we shouldn't have lost.

******

The rest of the day was spent tidying things up as the throng of onlookers on the quay and along the shoreline grew and grew—including a number of French knights who came galloping up about an hour later to confront us. It didn't do the French knights much good; it's hard to lower your visor and charge galleys full of archers. In any event, a long shot from one of our strongest archers hit one of the French horses and sent the knights hurrying away. It also temporarily scattered the crowd around them. The throng of Londoners quickly returned; the French never did.

It took quite some time to sort things out, and all the while people poured out of the city gates and the crowds along the river continued to grow until it became something of a festival. Onlookers crowded the quay and magicians, pickpockets, and women worked the crowd.

Whilst the festival was growing as more and more people arrived, we put the French wounded ashore so their friends could barber them and I told Peter to take his galley up to the bridge and make a reconnaissance to see how strongly it was being guarded. If he can take the bridge with minimal casualties, I told Peter, he was to do so and hold it until the army arrived, but he was to at all times keep his galley there so his landing party could quickly board it and escape if the French launched a serious counter attack.

If the bridge was heavily guarded, on the other hand, Peter was to return with his galley without trying to take it; if it was not heavily guarded and he was able to take it, he was to send his galley's dinghy back down the river to let me know. I particularly ordered him to keep his entire company near his galley if he took the bridge, and to at all times keep a clear escape path back to his galley—and not to under any circumstances leave a small force behind which might be overwhelmed by a counterattack.

Whilst Peter was gone upriver to check out the bridge, I boarded Richard Carpenter's galley and sent Harold with his galley and all of our prizes downstream to be anchored, all lashed together like a raft of logs, at the entrance to the river. Harold's entire galley company of archers went with him to guard them. We'll sort the prizes out and decide what to do with them later.

And then, of course, there was the inevitable unexpected problem. This one, however, was pleasant—a number of the French knights' large and apparently valuable horses were still on the lower deck of the horse transport. They would have to be fed and watered.

Hmm, I wonder what they would fetch if we sell them or if the French knights would pay to ransom them? Or perhaps we could trade them for more ambler mares. I'll have to ask Raymond and Freddy the hostler.

So what was the first order I gave after Harold and Peter hurried away?

"Tell the captains to bring all the rest of our galleys and anchor them just off this quay. We'll wait here on our galleys until we know the size of the enemy force Peter finds at the bridge."

Chapter Twenty-one

We're off to Windsor

"What now, Captain? Do we march up the river road past the Thames bridge or do we walk all the way around the city? And do we do it now or do we wait until it gets dark?"

The question was being asked of me over and over again, but for some reason I couldn't answer it or even see who was standing in the shadows talking to me. I kept trying to speak, but somehow I couldn't. Then I jerked awake and realized that someone was shaking my shoulder. It was John Small, my apprentice. I'd been dreaming behind my eyes.

"Lieutenant Commander Peter London's dinghy has just come down from the bridge with a message, Commandant. He says he has the bridge and can hold it."

"Good. That's very good," I said as I sat up and rubbed my eyes. It was dark and my neck was very stiff and sore. I must have twisted it when I was asleep.

"It means we can take the shorter route up the river road and go straight to Windsor." I added after a few more seconds of thought while I stretched my arms out and jiggled my hands in an effort to shake off my sleep.

Then I gave an order: "Summon the captains; we're going to row up to the bridge at first light and put the army ashore; we'll march to Windsor from there."

We hold the bridge so we could, of course, raise the bridge's drawbridge so our galleys' masts could pass through the bridge, and then try to row all the way up the river to Windsor. The river might well be deep enough. But we couldn't risk having the barons and French retake the bridge and cut off our galleys from the sea by preventing the drawbridge from being raised when they returned.

Our problem was quite straight forward; the men and the crews of the galleys could, and probably would, march home from Windsor if the French and the barons regained control of the bridge; but our galleys would almost certainly be lost if they couldn't get past the bridge to come back down the river."

The problem, of course, was how and where the French knights and their allies would respond if we attempted to march up the river road.

****** *William*

It was just after dawn when our galleys began simultaneously unloading their archers and their weapons and supplies all along the quay just downstream from the bridge over the Thames. Peter's men had the drawbridge up to accommodate the masts of our galleys in the event we wanted them to pass under the bridge and continue up the Thames, but we didn't. This was as far as our galleys would go; I wasn't about to risk having the French and barons cut them off from access to the sea.

The quay and the river near it was immediately the scene of intense activity with much shouting and running about. As soon as each galley's archers finished unloading, it pushed off to anchor in the river while we waited to see if it would be needed for a hurried evacuation if the expected French attack turned out to be stronger than we anticipated. The galleys would wait just off the quay until I gave the word for them to leave. Until I did, none of our galleys would be moving down the river to join Harold and our raft of prizes at the entrance to the Thames.

Neither the French nor the barons came out to challenge us as the heavily burdened archers from the first of our companies finished unloading their galley and began walking up the slippery stone steps from the road along the quay next to the bridge.

The archers carried their heavy loads of weapons, supplies, and arrow bales up the steps to the entrance to the bridge and then back down the steps on the other side, all the time looking about in absolute wonderment and curiosity at the great city and the bridge over the Thames. They were mostly country lads and this was the first time many of them had ever seen such a bridge or a big English city.

There was no sign of the French and the rebellious barons, and it certainly was not because they didn't know we were at the bridge and moving up the river road—the open area between the quay and the city wall was already filled with onlookers and more were constantly arriving despite the early hour. Could it be that our Jewish friends were wrong or the French knights had changed their minds about attacking us? The thought crossed my mind.

Once each company passed the entrance to the bridge and walked down the steps to reach the river road on the other side, it began marching with its rowing drums beating the step. It was quite a spectacle. The gathering mob of Londoners who stood and watched as we marched past seemed curious about the archers and impressed with all the weapons we were carrying and how we marched, but not particularly excited by the fact that we had defeated the French, at least no one called out to congratulate or thank us.

It was as if it was the spectacle of our arrival that interested the onlookers; the king's problems and the arrival of the French seemed to be of little concern, at least not so far as I could tell from the comments and shouts I overheard. Even so, several fights and heated arguments broke out in the rapidly growing crowd. I'm not sure what caused them and, truth be told, I didn't care.

As you might imagine, we made no effort to stop the fights or find out why they were occurring. It was likely the usual things that caused disturbances when crowds assembled in London—pickpockets, deceptive merchants, and women.

Peter's company, the company holding the bridge, fell in behind us as the last of the newly arrived archers came down the stone steps and began marching for Windsor to the beat of their rowing drums.

******

"I don't care what FitzWalter and the Earl of Devon think we should do; it's too dangerous to attack the king's mercenaries," Count du Bureau said to one of the French knights sitting at the table. "In the name of God, man, they of all people should know what a folly it would be to do so.

"Besides, we're stretched too thin as it is, even with the reinforcements that just arrived. If we lose too many more men we might not be able to hold the city's strongpoints, let alone its gates. Already some of our men have come down with the coughing pox caused by all the smoke and fog.

"My orders from Prince Louis are to hold London until he arrives, and that's what I intend to do. I'm not going to risk losing London by attacking mercenaries who are merely passing through on the roads outside of the city's walls and will be going back to Cornwall right after the meeting."

"Now, now, my Lords, there is no need for angry words," said the Pope's nuncio in a chiding but soothing voice as his assistants listened silently. "Surely there must be another way to send a message to King John and his supporters that the king is weak and would be better off abdicating in favour of Louis instead of being defeated and killed in a war."

"No, there isn't, Nuncio; no there isn't," said another French knight, a strong supporter of Prince Louis. "Destroying the mercenaries King John has hired to defend him is the only thing we can do to send the king the message that he must abdicate. If we don't destroy them, we must either go to war with John now before we are ready, or give up the fight for Louis to become king and let the barons agree to the charter."

The argument raged on and on for several hours.

In the end, after more than a few bowls of wine, du Bureau agreed that those of the French knights and men at arms who so desired could join the barons in attacking the archers as they marched to Windsor. He did so because he agreed with them that having the best fighting men was the key to success and the fighting in France last year had proved that the French knights were better than anyone else. Besides, if some of the fools got themselves killed there would be more English lands available for Louis to distribute and fewer Frenchmen to claim them.

He resolved to pass the thought on to his friends, but only his friends. He had earlier resolved not to give up London even if John reached an agreement with his barons.

****** *William*

We could still see the city walls of London and were making good time marching up the road along the Thames when the initial report came in from Peter that a large force of mounted men could be seen coming up the road behind us. I was at the head of our army at the time; Peter was bringing up the rear as the captain of our rear guard.

The report reached me in the usual way—the designated loud talker in each company shouted it to the loud talker in the company marching ahead of him, who then repeated it. A message sent thusly could sweep through our column in less than a minute.

I was already trotting hurriedly towards the rear of our column when the second order came down the column from Peter. *Deploy into battle position five facing rear.* Its meaning was clear to everyone; we were about to face a force of mounted knights approaching from the rear.

Our column immediately, and for the most part silently, began changing shape. Of course it did so silently. The men were forbidden from speaking under the pain of suffering harsh penalties if they did. Silence was necessary so that the orders of each company's captain could be clearly heard.

What the men of each company immediately did was what they'd been learnt and practiced many times before— follow their company's flag and form on it in battle position five when the flag stopped moving and started being waved in a tight circle.

Battle position five meant seven-deep files with the first three men in each file wielding a long-handled, hooked and bladed pike in addition to their longbow and the man carrying the anti-arrow shields standing seventh in the line with a gap of ten paces between the third and fourth man.

Every man knew what battle position five meant and where he should be as a result—it meant we were facing mounted knights and no archers. The gap between the third and fourth men was where a mounted knight might be expected to fall if his horse was stopped by one of our bladed pikes and the knight riding the horse wasn't.

If there had been archers accompanying the knights, it would be battle position six and the two men at the back of each file carrying large shields would move up to the front of the file and hold them up to protect the men behind them from arrows.

******

Peter and I stood in front of our men and watched the French knights who had stopped about five hundred paces in front of us. There were about a hundred of them, or perhaps a little more, and they were just out of arrow range. Behind us some of our men were still placing and sharpening their stakes. Everyone's bow was strung including mine and the bladed pikes and bales of extra arrows were already laid out on the ground so as to be instantly available.

"Do you think they know far we can push out an arrow with our longbows and are deliberately stay out of range, or are they just lucky? Peter asked to no one in particular.

"Lucky, I hope. But perhaps they know. What happened to FitzWalter and his men must surely be known to the French by now, wouldn't you think?"

"Well, we may be about to find out. Here comes someone."

An elegantly dressed rider on a magnificently caparisoned horse detached himself from the milling group of French knights and trotted up to us with some kind of special gait wherein the horse lifted its front hooves higher than normal. It was quite impressive.

"I am Robert du Mons from the college of heralds," the rider announced in French as he reached us and bowed down towards us from his saddle with a smile. "I am come to see if I can reconcile you with the knights of Prince Louis and, if I cannot reconcile you, to seek your agreement as how you should meet in battle and how the battle should be named. May I know your names and titles?"

It was the kind of formality one saw a tournament, or so I'd been told.

"My name is William and this is Peter. We are archers from Cornwall marching to join King John of England. As I'm sure you know, we've been contracted to defend the king for six months or until he reaches an agreement with his dissident barons" … "and their supporters," I added with a smile and a nodding bow of my head towards the French knights milling about in the distance.

I saw no men on foot so there was no need to goad the French horse into an immediate mounted attack by insulting their bravery. To the contrary, I would have preferred no attack at all.

"We have no reason to fight the highly esteemed knights of Prince Louis," I said quite pleasantly and most friendly.

"Our destination is Windsor and we would prefer to march there in peace. But if we are set upon by yon knights, we will fight; and if we fight we will offer no quarter to those who attack us, accept no surrenders, and say no prayers for Prince Louis's dead when we strip them of their weapons and armour and tip their bodies into a ditch to rot."

"I shall convey your thoughts to Prince Louis's men," the herald agreed with a nod and a suddenly sober-appearing face. He was obviously taken aback; those were clearly not the tournament terms of knights and nobles.

"Those are not our thoughts," I responded coolly as Peter nodded his agreement. "Those are our commitments."

******

Peter and I walked back to the front of our army's battle formation as the herald rode back to the assembling French. We were ready to fight with each of our seven companies in position with its captain and his lieutenant standing in front of their men so they could be seen and their men would know they hadn't been abandoned.

Everyone was watching as I started to wave my hand in a circle over my head to summon them, and then thought better of it. Instead, Peter and I hurried to each of the companies to give its captain his orders in person so we could see for ourselves that the captain's company was ready to receive the imminent French attack. But first I needed to piss. So I lifted my tunic and that's what I did—to the accompaniment of a great roar of approval from my men as I aimed my water towards the French.

Then Peter and I went from company to company and I gave its captain the same order in a voice loud enough for the men of his company to hear.

"Pass the word to your men that the French knights are going to attack us for no good reason except to harm us, so we're going to treat them as we would treat pirates; we're not taking prisoners."

What Peter and I saw as each company got its "no prisoners" order was encouraging. Our men were as ready as we could get them. They all had their stakes set, their arrows nocked, and their arrow bales untied and in their proper places. The men in the first three lines had their pikes and positioned out of sight on the ground with their butt holes dug; those in the next four lines had their short swords and shields on the ground next to them and ready to be instantly picked up and used.

We had barely finished our brief meetings with the captains and resumed our places when the French riders began to move forward, first at a walk, and then at a trot with their visors closed. They were all carrying lances as if they in one of their tournaments. *What fools.* I waited with my hand raised as far as it would go until the bulk of the French riders had trotted far enough towards us that I thought they were in our killing zone.

All along in front of companies the captains and lieutenants had their arms similarly raised and were watching me intently. So, for that matter, were all the archers in our formation who were standing in a position from which they could see me. Preparing to receive an enemy attack was something we had all done many times in our war games; this time, however, it was for real.

******

I dropped my hand, shouted "push" as loudly as I could, and stepped back into my position in our battle formation to add my arrows to those that were already in the air. All around me as I did, I could hear the grunts of the archers as they pushed out their arrows and the "push" … "push" cries of the sergeants and chosen men.

The effect of the continuous storm of arrows falling on the French knights and their horses was instantaneous: horses bolted in every direction and a handful of men and horses immediately fell—and a substantial number of the French knights began charging towards us.

The heavily armoured French knights were brave; I'll say that for them. And they were also rather stupid and poorly led since they made no effort to curve around and hit us from the side or rear. They just lowered their visors and behaved as if they were in a tournament—they charged straight ahead through the constant storm of arrows that fell on them like a downpour of rain from sky.

It was their horses who were particularly vulnerable, not the heavily armoured knights. Horses just do not react well when an arrow sticks them. Some of the charging French knights' horses were hit and stopped charging towards us as they tumbled head over hoofs or bolted in an agonized panic despite the best efforts of their riders to control them.

The falling knights and horses, in turn, caused those behind them to trip over them and fall. Others of the French knights pulled up their horses and turned back before they reached our stakes rather than attempt to ride their horses through them; others, however, perhaps half of the French knights, had either not seen the thicket of sharpened stakes set out in front of our battle line or had not understood what they meant. They rode their horses straight into them just as they would at a tournament.

In the end, very few of the French knights reached our front line and most of those who did never saw the pikes come up that impaled their horses and sent them flying.

Chapter Twenty-two

We receive visitors

We spent the rest of the day finishing off the fallen French knights and stripping them of their clothes and armour. Some of what they'd been wearing and carrying was quite nice and would fetch a good price after it was patched and cleaned up a bit. Wains traveling on the nearby road were soon hired to carry our handful of dead to the next church cemetery along the road and our wounded men and loot to the archers' camp near Windsor.

John Small and Peter's apprentice had both been ordained by Thomas so they gobbled the church words necessary to send our unlucky dead on their way to heaven while the rest of us stood in our ranks with our heads bowed and muttered "amen" each time the Latin gobbler prompted us by lifting his hand in a "give me" gesture. Immediately afterwards we continued on our march to Windsor.

What we didn't do was throw the French dead in a ditch as I had promised; we didn't have time to waste so we just stripped them and left them where they lay for the birds who were already gathering. Perhaps the French who ran away will come back and bury them.

******

King John had already heard about our victories over Devon and Spencer and the rumours reaching Windsor about our latest victories over the French had excited him even more. It convinced him he would be safe if he temporarily left the castle with a strong force to guard him. As a result, he and a great gaggle of his courtiers decided to ride out of Windsor to congratulate us and associate themselves with our successes.

And, of course, the sight of what appeared to be a band of knights galloping down the Thames road towards us resulted in our army rapidly deploying into a defensive formation and preparing to greet them with a shower of arrows and raised pikes.

The confusion was overcome without anyone being killed and a smiling King John was soon walking along our hastily formed battle line and talking as if he had somehow been personally involved in the victories of Harold's galleys and Peter's army by "inspiring" their men. We, of course, encouraged his delusions with blatantly nonsensical lies such as "your majesty's your name was repeatedly shouted by the men while they were fighting." He was very pleased and seemed to actually believe it.

On the other hand, there was also a dark side to the king's unexpected appearance: William Marshal was among the courtiers who had ridden out with the king to visit us— and he had seen everything including our rapid move into a battle formation and our modern weapons. Marshal was pensive and reflective as he stood behind the babbling king amongst the smiling courtiers.

So far as I was concerned, and my lieutenants agreed later that evening, Marshal's presence was more than little unfortunate, it was a damn disaster. His knowledge as to how we organized our battle lines and how we were armed was a problem that could hurt us in the future when our relations with the king might not be so favourable.

Worse, Marshal was smart behind his eyes; I sensed that he understood what he had seen and the implications of our constant training and modern weapons—and that understanding was the very thing he would need to know if he was ever to prepare an army and lead it against us.

The rest of the excitement surrounding the king's visit was not so worrisome. For one, I had a fine and unexpected family reunion and received much encouraging news. My son George, my brother Thomas, Raymond, and George's schoolboy friend, Richard, the young four-stripe captain of Raymond's outriders, had also ridden out to congratulate us. They arrived immediately after King John and his courtiers and brought George's small band of surviving horse archers with them.

George and Richard and their five horse archers, my son explained to me, had come to Windsor with Thomas several days earlier from Oxford to report their victory over the knights and village levies of a rebel baron by the name of Spencer. It seems that Spencer and over a hundred of his men had attacked George and his heavily outnumbered horse archers whilst they were stopped at a tavern on the London road, captured and murdered three of George's men, and then had been soundly defeated by the surviving handful of horse archers as evidenced by the wain full of bloody armour, weapons, and equipment they had brought into Windsor as prizes.

As a result of coming to Windsor to report the horse archers' victory over Spencer and his men, George and Thomas had heard of the fighting between the archers and the French on the Thames, and then again outside the city walls. When they heard we were marching up the Thames road to join the king and that the king was riding out to welcome us, they decided to follow along and join in welcoming us.

I was greatly moved by what George and Richard had accomplished and immediately awarded another stripe to every one of the seven survivors of the fight with Spencer's army. Not to be outdone when he heard the cheering that resulted and inquired about it, the king immediately knighted George, Richard, Raymond, and Peter and promised to do the same for Henry and Harold. Then he got bored and left. It seems he wanted to get back to Windsor in time to have a meal with the queen and a good night's sleep so he'd be well rested when he went hunting in the morning in Windsor forest with his friends.

His courtiers clattered away behind him.

It was an altogether great and momentous day except that now the commander of the king's army knew about our bladed pikes and how we organize ourselves to use them and our longbows when we fight on land. That, of course, is all the more reason why we should greatly increase the number of horse archers in England—so we can conduct our battles differently if we have to fight in England in the years ahead.

Raymond was always asking for more men and horses so I knew he'd be pleased when I tell him that we'd be doubling the number of horse archers under his command and stationing a new company at Launceston and another at Trematon. Hopefully, the foot archers outside of England will also grow and be able to bring in enough additional coins to support the two new companies of horse archers and continue to add to the ever growing number of coins in the chests at Restormel.

But first, of course, before I announce the expansion, I must follow our custom and consult with my available lieutenants.

******

The next morning Peter marched his army to Windsor to link up with Henry and our companies who were already there. Thomas, George, Raymond, and I, however, rode directly to Runnymede to see the site where the king would be meeting with the barons in a few days' time. Richard and the newly promoted horse archers came with us. I wanted to see it immediately even though we would all return the next day with Henry and Peter to see it again and begin finalizing our plans to guard the king during his visit.

What we found when we reached Runnymede was a somewhat deserted meadow near the Thames where three sets of tents had been being erected with banners flying from them. One group of tents had been pitched at the Windsor end of the meadow for the king and his representatives; another group had been set up at the Staines end of the meadow for the barons; and a third set in the middle of the meadow where the king and the barons and their representatives would meet.

There was a lot of activity around the barons' tents, but nowhere elsewhere in the meadow.

Langton's plan, according to Thomas was the parties, or their representatives, to come each day to this neutral ground from their respective camps—the king and his supporters from Windsor; the barons from Staines. We, of course, would be marching with the king each day to protect him and help demonstrate his power.

Our arrival set off a chain of events. We were newly arrived and still sitting on our horses deep in conversation when a tonsured priest hurried across the meadow from the barons' tents with a self-important look on his face and demanded to know who we were and what we are doing. He spoke English with a pronounced French accent. Thomas was wearing his archers' tunic instead of his bishop's clothes or perhaps the priest would not have been so demanding.

Hmm. I wonder which side he's on?

"Just looking, Father, just looking." Thomas assured the priest.

"Looking isn't allowed; I'm afraid I have to ask you to leave immediately," was the priest's prissily delivered response with a "shooing" motion of his hands as if we some kind of bug from the river.

I became quite irritable behind my eyes at hearing the priest's dismissive words. There is no other way to describe it. For some reason he reminded me of the village priest I had hated so much when I was a lad.

"We're not leaving," I said with a rather cool tone in my voice as I leaned towards the priest with a scowl and made the same insulting "shooing" motion back at him to send him away. "So go away."

The priest took one look at my scarred and battered face and hurriedly turned away to march, yes march, with great determination and self-importance towards what I presumed to be the barons' tents as they were at the edge of the meadow closest to Staines where the rebel barons had their encampment.

Thomas and I stayed mounted but Raymond, George, and most of the archers climbed down to stretch their legs as we continued talking and gesturing amongst ourselves about such things as where in the meadow our men might be positioned to best defend themselves and do the necessaries such as piss and shite while the king parleyed with the barons. We were not alone for long.

*****

"Uh oh. Here come's trouble," Thomas said as he leaned to the side of his horse to press the tip of his longbow against the ground and bend it so he could slide to loop at the end his bowstring into the notch at the end of his bow.

A dozen or so armed men were walking across the meadow towards us from the area of the barons' tents. Their determination to confront us was instantly evident from the way they were walking.

I leaned over and strung my bow and, without a word being spoken, so did the archers around us who were standing in the meadow next to their horses or relaxing in their saddles. I'm not sure the men walking to us with such determined strides were close enough to see us string our bows or, if they did, they understood what it meant. Perhaps they were bold and determined because the priest reported, quite correctly, that we weren't carrying swords and shields and they were.

Not a word was spoken as the men approached with their determination to deal with us showing in every step. We just stood there silently and watched them come to us. One of George's veterans quietly swung up on to his horse to get closer to the arrows in the quivers draped across his horse's shoulders in front of his saddle.

"You were told to leave," the burly leader of the group said as he walked up to us. He was almost as tall as George and about ten years older with a much longer beard and well dressed, almost certainly a knight of some sort. Like the priest, he spoke English with a French accent.

He was carrying a long sword strapped to his back and holding a shield in his left hand, but he didn't appear to be wearing chain under his tunic. The men behind him appeared to be similarly armed and unprotected. Some of them had their swords on their backs as their captain did; others were holding them in one hand and their shields in the other.

"So we were; so we were," I replied with an agreeable nod of my head. "And who might you be and whose men are you—the barons', the king's or Langton's? Not that it makes much difference, but I'm curious."

"Never you mind about that, just get you gone." Then the leader of men confronting us, whoever he was, made the mistake of reaching over his shoulder and starting to pull his sword. It was a fatal mistake; I never did like arrogant men telling me what to do and pulling a sword to threaten me was just too much. I reached over my shoulder as I had many thousands of times before in battle and practice, and in one continuous move nocked my arrow and pushed it on its way.

The man's sword hadn't even begun to clear its sheath when the arrow took him. He staggered back a step or two and his eyes widened in shock and surprise as he saw the fletching feathers of the arrow sticking out of his chest. He couldn't see the point of the arrow sticking at least a foot out of his back, but the men standing behind him certainly could.

"No more," I shouted to my men at the same moment as I pushed my arrow into the arrogant knight. "One's enough."

The men who had approached us with such ferocious determination seemed to be frozen in place for several blinks of their eyes; then they turned and ran for their lives. We stood without speaking and watched them go.

The dead man's legs were still trembling when I dismounted and had my men throw him across the saddle of my horse. He stopped kicking as I casually led my horse and my men towards the barons' tents at the end of the field. One of George's men walked on each side of my horse to keep the knight's body from sliding off, the rest were mounted and rode easy behind us.

A crowd of several dozen of men stopped working and came out to watch as we slowly approached in a peaceful and non-threatening manner with me leading the horse carrying the dead man. There were three or four priests among the men who waited for us and several were dressed such that they might be knights or nobles. All of my men were mounted except the three of us bringing the dead man to his friends. No one said a word as we walked up.

"The next man who draws a sword on the archers of Cornwall will die even faster than this one," I said as I reached the wide-eyed and speechless waiting crowd, and tipped the dead man off my horse. He slid off head first and landed with a thud in a clump of high grass next to one of the barons' tents. The shaft of my arrow snapped and cloud of seeds and dust rose around the dead man as he hit the ground face first and rolled over.

"Whose man do you think he was? I asked Thomas as I mounted up and we turned our horses towards Windsor.

Chapter Twenty-three

Runnymede

Three days later we formed up into a column of sixteen companies of foot archers and waited for the king and his supporters to ride out of the castle to join us. He was so late that Peter wondered aloud if he had changed his mind.

If he ever arrived, the plan was for all sixteen galley companies of foot archers to march in a seven-man wide column to the Runnymede meadow where the king would meet the barons and accept the "articles of the barons" which listed their demands. It was June 10th and all of the foot archers including myself were on foot. Only Raymond and his horse archers were mounted.

The king was late in coming out of his castle and would, as a result, be late to his meeting with the barons. We were ready and had been waiting for some time even though his late arrival had been expected. According to Thomas, the king and his advisors thought his being late would help convince the rebel barons of the king's power and importance. I wasn't so sure of that even though the men appreciated his absence; it gave them a chance to sit around idly in the sun to piss when they want to do so and tell each other stories. In any event, he was significantly late.

When King John finally rode up to where we were patiently waiting, he was accompanied by William Marshal and a great gaggle of the king's loyal knights and barons, all with their banners flying and all of them trying to get close to the king in an effort to gain his recognition by indicating their willingness to fight to protect him.

It was a great, colourful, and rather impressive and disorganized army of men whose horses trotted down the road to the long column of archers waiting on the road below the castle. A galley's company of archers could have easily taken the whole lot.

When everyone was assembled and ready, we set off for Runnymede with the companies of marching foot archers leading the way followed by the king and his supporters. Raymond and his horse archers brought up the rear.

The foot archers marched carrying all of their weapons and all of their bales of extra arrows. We were fully ready and organized to fight and rightly so—because, as every veteran soldier knows, the best way to prevent an enemy from attacking you is to be ready to kill him if he does.

I walked at the very front of the column with my newly promoted son walking by my side; Henry and Peter walked at the middle of the column so they could split off and lead the second half of our army, eight full galley companies of foot archers, into the Runnymede meadow in a separate column marching parallel to the eight companies I was leading so there would be about three hundred paces between the two columns of archers.

Our entrance into the meadow was quite impressive and the barons and their retainers all came out to watch. We marched seven abreast to the beat of our drums as we led the way for the king and his loyal knights and barons, all with their banners flying, riding close behind him.

Arriving in the meadow in two columns and marching them about three hundred paces apart right up to the great meeting tent in the middle of the meadow was my idea. It would enable the king and his supporters to ride safely to the meeting tent through the open area between our two columns—both whom merely needed to stop and make a half turn in either direction to be in our favoured seven-men-deep battle formation and ready to fight.

******

The king rode to the meeting on his large and beautifully caparisoned horse, with his great banner flying and a great gaggle of his loyal supporters following close behind. He was impressively kingly and regal as he rode down the lane between the two columns of archers to the central meeting tent where he would formally accept the "Articles of the Barons," the list of rights the barons demanded the king surrender to them.

The rebellious barons and the king's representatives and advisors were already assembled and watching intently as our companies marched to the meeting tent to the beat of their drums and the king and his men entered the meadow.

We didn't know it at the time, of course, but the organized nature of the archers' arrival dismayed the barons and their men. They had never seen such a thing as an army marching together on the same foot to the beat of a drum. It suddenly dawned on some of them that the archers of Cornwall might be better organized and more dangerous than they had realized, and they might lose their lives and lands if they attacked the king while he was under their protection.

"Better to wait until they're gone" was the phrase increasingly heard as the meeting progressed in the days that followed and the barons discussed and argued with each other and the French about what to do next—sign or fight.

******

Ten days later, on another fine June day, we again marched to Runnymede when the king returned to sign the agreement surrendering some of his powers and accept the barons' renewed pledges of allegiance. The only thing different on our second march to Runnymede was that the king insisted that this time the captain of each of our marching companies must ride ahead of it on a horse "because it is more dignified and will impress the barons as to the abilities of our captains." He gifted us twenty horses from the Windsor stables for the purpose.

The problem, of course, was that none of the captains of our sixteen galley companies of foot archers had ever been on a horse before, and would be more likely than not to fall off if anything caused his horse to bolt or it decided to return to the stables to eat. We solved that problem by having each of our galley captains continue to march in his usual place at the head of his galleys' company of foot archers, with one of the horse archers riding the king's gift horse ahead of them and pretending to be the galley's captain.

The king's plan to demonstrate to the barons that his forces were well captained was a spectacular success when we once again marched into the meadow to the beat of our drums and the king rode in safety and splendour between our ranks to the meeting tent—not one of our faux captains fell off his horse to ruin the king's majesty, the barons signed and once again pledged their loyalties.

King John was justifiably proud of his idea to mount the galley captains on horses to impress the rebellious barons, and, as one might expect, was greatly applauded by his courtiers who quickly recognized the king's great wisdom and vied with each other to pronounce themselves to be in awe of it.

We left immediately for Cornwall with our new horses and all our prizes as soon as we got the king safely back to Windsor with his copy of the agreement.

End of the Book

The story is not over.

The charter signed by the king and the barons was immediately ignored by everyone who signed it even though it subsequently became known as the Magna Carta and became famous because it was the first time a king had agreed to surrender some of his powers to people he considered to be beneath him.

William and most of his archers didn't learn for quite some time that the agreement was being ignored and fighting had broken out again—because a few months after the signing William led most of the archers back to the Holy Land and the ports in and around the Mediterranean to resume earning their coins and bread carrying refugees and cargos in their cogs and galleys. They'd be back.

Please read more.

All of the other action-packed books in this great saga of medieval England are also available as eBooks and some are available in print. You can find them by going to Amazon or Google and searching for *Martin Archer fiction*. A collection of the first six books of the saga is available on Kindle as *The Archers' Story*. Similarly, a collection of the next four books in the saga is available as *The Archers' Story: Part II*, and there are additional books beyond those four.

And a word from Martin:

I hope you enjoyed reading *The Magna Carta* as much as I enjoyed writing it. If so, I respectfully request a favourable review on Amazon and elsewhere with as many stars as possible in order to encourage other readers. And I would also very much like to know your thoughts about the story. I can be reached at martinarcherV@gmail.com. /S/ Martin Archer

Amazon eBooks in the exciting and action-packed *The Company of Archers* saga:

The Archers

The Archers' Castle

The Archers' Return

The Archers' War

Rescuing the Hostages

Kings and Crusaders

The Archers' Gold

The Missing Treasure

Castling the King

The Sea Warriors

The Captain's Men

Gulling the Kings

The Magna Carta Decision

Fires in the Distance (coming)

Amazon eBooks in Martin Archer's exciting and action-packed *Soldier and Marines* saga:

Soldier and Marines

Peace and Conflict

War Breaks Out

War in the East

Israel's Next War

Collections

The Archer's Story - books I, II, III, IV, V, VI

The Archer's Story II - books VII, VIII, IX, X,

Soldiers and Marines Trilogy

Other eBooks you might enjoy:

Cage's Crew by Martin Archer writing as Raymond Casey

America's Next War by Michael Cameron – an adaption of *War Breaks Out* to set it in our immediate future.

———————————————

Made in the USA
Coppell, TX
05 March 2025

46737042R00146